He felt an uncharacteristic eagerness to be close to her

She smelled so good. And her body felt so delicate in his arms.

Instead of crushing her lips and plundering her mouth as he wanted, he forced his lips to trail down her jaw to the safer territory of her smooth brown neck.

Only now he was immersed in her scent, and it clouded his already hazy mind. He couldn't resist the urge to lick the indent at the base of her neck, and it immediately constricted with her gasp of pleasure.

Her hands dipped to the small of his back just above the waistband of his jeans. Taking that as encouragement, he let his hips rock against hers, knowing she'd feel the full extent of his excitement.

Leaning into him, Shelly raised her lips to his once again. Finally, she seemed to have let go of her inhibitions and was taking the lead.

Books by Robyn Amos

Kimani Romance

Enchanting Melody
Sex and the Single Braddock
Cosmic Rendezvous

Kimani Arabesque

Promise Me
I Do!
Private Lies
Into the Night
True Blue

ROBYN AMOS

worked a multitude of day jobs while pursuing a career in writing after graduating from college with a degree in psychology. Then she married her real-life romantic hero, a genuine rocket scientist and she was finally able to live her dream of writing full-time. Since her first book was published in 1997, Robyn has written tales of romantic comedy and suspense for several publishers, including Harlequin Books, Kensington Books and HarperCollins. A native of the Washington, D.C., metropolitan area, Robyn currently resides in Odenton, Maryland.

Cosmic Rendezvous

Robyn Amos

KIMANI
ROMANCE

This book is for Gretchen England. Thanks for letting
me steal pieces of your life for this book.
Remember me when you get into space one day!

KIMANI PRESS™

Recycling programs
for this product may
not exist in your area.

ISBN-13: 978-0-373-86108-8
ISBN-10:   0-373-86108-7

COSMIC RENDEZVOUS

Copyright © 2009 by Robyn Amos

www.kimanipress.com

Printed in U.S.A.

Dear Reader,

My husband is an aerospace engineer, and therefore, so are many of our friends. I got the idea for *Cosmic Rendezvous* when one of those friends announced that she was moving to Houston to train astronauts on a new vehicle that will soon replace the space shuttle. A bunch of us were sitting around a table playing Texas Hold 'Em and joking that my friend would move to Texas and marry a cowboy. But not just any cowboy…a *space* cowboy. That's when Lincoln "Lightning" Ripley was born—Mr. Right Stuff himself.

I had a great time researching this book because my husband took a real interest in helping me with the technical aspects. We visited Houston with the double mission of catching up with my friend and touring Johnson Space Center. We dined in a pub where astronauts go to hang out and viewed the underwater lab where they simulate a weightless environment. I also learned that the Houston humidity is hard on a woman's hair. Hopefully I was able to bring all of those experiences to life in this book.

Shelly and Linc have a tough road to travel to find their happy ending. But in *Cosmic Rendezvous,* they eventually discover that no amount of stubbornness, stress or catastrophes can stand in the path of true love.

I love to hear from readers. E-mail me at robynamos@aol.com or visit me on the Web at www.robynamos.com.

Happy reading,

Robyn Amos

Chapter 1

Shelly London shifted her stare from the blinking error message on her monitor to the window and back again. She was tempted to hoist her computer through the glass and jump out after it.

Moving to Houston to train astronauts on an experimental spacecraft for NASA wasn't nearly as cool as it had originally seemed.

She'd felt as though she'd been caught up in a tornado from the minute she'd stepped off the plane from Washington, D.C. Between setting up her new home and overseeing the final design and production of the spacecraft, she'd barely had a moment to herself.

And there certainly hadn't been time to find a decent hairdresser, she thought, patting her gel-slicked topknot. Houston's humidity had gotten the best of her, and it had been one bad-hair day after another.

She knew her life would never resemble a rerun of *Sex and the City*. Expensive clothes and shoes, fabulous parties with beautiful people and an endless string of handsome men weren't her destiny.

But at least back in D.C., she'd been stylish and put together, making the most of her cute potential. She'd had a social life, with girlfriends and dates when she'd wanted them, and close family ties with her mother and sister. Shelly knew it would take some time to build a life here in Houston, but it was slower going than she'd expected.

Still living out of boxes, she was lucky to put together a shirt and pants that matched. This made it easy to fall into the collegelike culture of her fellow aerospace geeks. Rolling out of bed for shift work, she dressed in blue jeans and old T-shirts, and ate whatever fast food was available.

She was close with those on her engineering team— most of whom she'd brought with her from D.C.—and knew the affable group of guys couldn't care less how she looked. But just once since she'd moved to Houston, she'd like to have a good-hair day.

Yesterday, out of a desperate need for a touch-up, she'd pulled off the highway and walked into a hair salon. She'd figured that with the name Lady of Color, she had a fighting chance of getting a stylist who could straighten her frizzled mess. She'd been right about one thing. The salon did specialize in African-American hair. Unfortunately, it didn't specialize in doing it well.

Shelly's hair had been bone straight when she left the salon yesterday, but that had lasted only until she walked through the thick, souplike humidity to her car this morning. By the time she'd driven to her office—with the windows down, because the air conditioner was broken—she'd looked like a wet poodle.

After two months and two containers of hair gel, Shelly had been looking forward to sporting something other than a bun or an unruly ponytail. No such luck. Thanks to the emergency gel she'd retrieved from the trunk of her car and the wide rubber band from her desk drawer, she was back to her perpetual bad-hair-day look.

In fact, it was looking as if it was going to be a bad day all the way around. In the dark monitor of her computer, which she was rebooting for the third time, she saw the reflection of a thunderstorm headed her way. Actually, it was Lightning. Lightning Ripley.

But she refused to use Lincoln Ripley's self-indulgent nickname out loud. Shelly didn't care how many engineers on her team suffered from hero worship. Or how often she heard women in the ladies' room drooling over his chiseled features and rock-hard muscles. Shelly was convinced Ripley's reputation was all hype.

By her estimation, he was a cocky, overconfident hotshot, channeling Will Smith in *Independence Day*. Ripley thought he was a hero destined to become a legend, and Shelly didn't want any part of it.

Guardian Rescue Mission, or GRM, was her baby. Draco, the spacecraft, was *her* design. And she wasn't going to let some ego-driven astronaut ruin the very thing her entire career and reputation were riding on.

Spinning around in her chair to face him, Shelly braced herself. She knew exactly what was coming. And it wasn't going to be pretty.

* * *

Lincoln Ripley felt anger radiating from his body like invisible waves of heat. He stalked up to Shelly London, fully intending to spin her chair to face him, but she stole his thunder when she turned to him on her own.

She stopped him short with the look of challenge in her dark eyes. He knew right then that she was going to be trouble. He wished for some way to wipe that smug expression off her face.

"Who the hell do you think you are? You don't have the authority to get me pulled off this mission." At the sound of his voice echoing through the quiet room, three heads popped up in alarm. The rest of the team was watching the scene with rapt attention, but Linc didn't care.

Shelly stared up at him without blinking. Her cold gaze sent a shiver down his spine. "You *haven't* been pulled from the mission. So, what's the problem?"

Linc blinked. Was she kidding? That morning she'd issued a request to the mission director for his reassignment. "The problem is that you *tried* to get me kicked off."

"Relax, Ripley. This isn't *Survivor*. You can't be voted off, as you well know. I simply inquired as to whether you were the best choice for lead astronaut on this mission."

Her indifference ramped up his anger another notch. "You question whether or not I'm the best choice? Don't you know who I am?"

His stomach muscles were clenched. Linc was used to maintaining his composure, especially with women. He couldn't remember the last time he'd reacted this strongly to one.

More infuriating was that her cool smile never changed. "Sure. You're a lieutenant colonel in the United States Air Force."

Linc ground his teeth together. She was being deliberately obtuse. "And…"

She gave an unladylike snort. "Oh, you want to know if I saw you on the covers of *Time*, *Newsweek* and *People*. Yes, I'm well aware of your reputation," she said irreverently. "But piloting a space shuttle has nothing to do with flying Draco. And I'm only interested in training astronauts who are focused on this mission rather than their own achievements."

Linc suppressed a curse. *His achievements had won him an Airman's Medal.* His body had now grown so hot, it was only a matter of time before steam poured from his ears.

"I can't believe your nerve—"

"There seems to be plenty of nerve to go around, because you had the nerve to miss my briefing yesterday."

Linc pounded the desk with his fist. "Is that what this is about? Missing one lousy meeting?"

Her back straightened, and for the first time, Linc spotted a crack in her composure. "No, this isn't about one lousy meeting. I didn't see you in the Mojave Desert when Draco was unveiled four months ago, and you didn't show up for the first round of flight testing, either."

His gut clenched. He'd missed those dates because he'd been flying a covert rescue mission out of Iraq. But he couldn't discuss that with a civilian. He had no choice but to take the hit to his reputation. "It was my understanding that those exercises were optional."

"Now we're down to the wire, and training is about to begin. Yesterday's briefing was *not* optional, and you weren't there. Draco is my design. I don't want anyone on the team who doesn't take the spacecraft just as seriously as I do."

He'd had enough of her attitude. "*Your* design. Important to *you*. Lady, this mission isn't *about* you. GRM is a top-secret *military* operation. Missing one little meeting doesn't warrant you trying to get me bumped from the mission."

"The briefing wasn't one little meeting. It was *the* meeting. And because you weren't at *the* meeting, you don't know anything about this spacecraft. It's a new design that you've never seen before. This mission is on a rushed deadline. We don't have time to waste catching you up whenever you decide your Porsche needs detailing."

"It's a 1969 Cobra, and it needed a carburetor." He'd nearly killed himself in that car trying to get to the meeting on time, but his pride wouldn't let him tell her that.

She rolled her eyes. "Whatever. In any case, you're still on the project. It's no secret that I'm not thrilled about that fact, but we have to work together, nonetheless. So, if you're through disrupting the room, those of us who actually work here have to get back to it." She spun her chair back around to face her computer.

Linc just stood there for a moment, staring incredulously. There were a million things he could have said, and would have said, if he weren't so confused.

She'd just dismissed him. No woman had ever dismissed Lincoln Ripley.

Once Shelly heard Linc finally leave the room, she released the breath she'd been holding. That man infuriated her.

She was so mad, she was nearly shaking, but she hadn't wanted him to see that. Shelly couldn't focus on her computer screen. Sucking in a deep breath, she pulled her glasses off. She missed her contacts, but she still hadn't found the time to find an optometrist to update her prescription.

Lately, there wasn't time for anything the least bit personal. There certainly wasn't time for a social life of any kind. And to make matters worse, because her mission was top-secret, she couldn't talk to her family about what she was doing. That made for some strained conversations, because work had become her life.

But it would be worth it. All her life, Shelly had wanted to be an astronaut. Even now as an aerospace engineer, she'd applied to the astronaut program three times. And she'd been rejected. Three times.

After her last rejection, she'd begun to doubt herself. But her boss had given her another shot when he recommended her to work on Draco. He'd told her that this could be her ticket to the stars. And with that goal in mind, Shelly had worked hard on the project. Her ideas for the vehicle had been innovative enough that she'd eventually become the lead designer.

Unfortunately, when that phase had been completed, and she'd angled for a slot on the spacecraft as an expert on the design and maintenance, Shelly had been shot down again. It was at that point that they'd been informed that this new spacecraft was for a military operation that would be manned solely by military personnel.

This wasn't unusual. Many of NASA's astronauts were pulled directly from the military, particularly the Air Force, since jet flight experience was valued so highly. But, Shelly knew her background in aerospace engineering should have made her sufficiently qualified under normal circumstances.

Every move Shelly had made in her career was to prepare her to become an astronaut. NASA relied heavily on its private contractors, and Shelly had gone to work for Welloney Incorporated straight from graduate school because they held contracts for some of NASA's most high-profile projects.

When she learned GRM wasn't going to get her into space, Shelly had almost thrown in the towel then and there, but there had been a silver lining. For her hard work on the project, she'd been promoted and sent to Houston to train the astronauts on Draco. It was hardly the next best thing to riding a rocket into space, but the money was good, and Shelly needed a change.

She'd be damned if she'd sit back and watch some hotshot pilot take Draco for granted. If she couldn't man the craft herself, she at least wanted astronauts that saw the mission as more than another notch in their belts.

Shelly shook her head over the argument she'd just had. He'd been trying to intimidate her. Lincoln Ripley was clearly the kind of man who was used to having his way.

Why else would he have leaned over her like that? He'd probably expected that she would get a lungful of that designer cologne he wore and swoon. Or maybe he'd thought she'd be mesmerized by his chocolate-brown eyes and offer him whatever he asked for.

This was the first time Shelly had seen Linc up close, and she couldn't deny, he was every bit as handsome as the rumor mill suggested. The women in the administration office called him Mr. Right Stuff. But that little fact only annoyed her more.

She hated men like him. The kind that never had to work hard at anything. Panties dropped at their feet with a glance, they made touchdowns without breaking a sweat, and their egos... Shelly was surprised Linc could keep a plane in the air with the weight of his ego on board.

No, this wasn't the kind of astronaut she wanted on her mission, but they were stuck with each other. Yet, if Lincoln Ripley thought he was going to bat his thick eyelashes and get what he wanted from her, he was sorely mistaken.

She was in charge, and she wasn't going to let him forget it.

Two days later, Linc was still trying to figure out what he was going to do about Shelly London. It seemed she'd set her mind on riding him hard.

He smiled at the double entendre. If she were any other woman, he might try making the other meaning of that statement a reality. But Linc couldn't get past her hard edge long enough to see her that way. Prim updo. Glasses. She was clearly wound too tight. And Linc liked his women soft and loose.

At first, he hadn't known why she was dead set against him, but he'd been certain it was an opinion she'd formed long before they'd ever met.

Sure, from the outside looking in, it might seem to her that flying her spacecraft wasn't a priority to him—an assumption that couldn't be further from the truth. But his gut told him that was just a surface excuse for her to *continue* despising him.

Linc had to admit, having a woman hate him on sight was a new sensation, and it had thrown him off his game for a minute. But he'd never been one to run from a challenge.

So what if she didn't want him piloting Draco? Colonel Murphy, the mission director, had made it clear that losing him wasn't an option.

His next move had been to turn the tables on her. If she didn't want to work with him, why couldn't she go back to Washington and turn the work over to the remaining team members? After all, Draco was nearly built. What did they need her for now?

He needed to know exactly what kind of enemy he was up against in Shelly. That meant finding out whatever he could about her.

Getting information out of her engineering team had been easy. They were a bit starstruck in his presence and were eager to answer his questions. From them, he'd learned that she was as hard to ditch from this mission as he was.

He hadn't placed much weight on her words when she'd bragged about designing Draco. Spacecrafts were designed by teams, and being the project manager didn't exactly make her a genius.

Except in this case. Apparently, she had been a junior member of the design team and had graduated to PM based on her development of a system that could increase propulsion while reducing fuel usage. It was technology that had never been seen before, making Shelly the absolute authority.

Using that fact as leverage, Shelly had lobbied to be included on the flight team as an engineer. Of course, she hadn't had a chance in hell of that happening. Draco would only be boarded by military personnel. That was a mandate that had come from the vice president himself.

Linc had spent the better part of his morning grilling engineers, but at least now he'd figured out why Shelly had it out for him. She wanted to be an astronaut. And she probably resented him because he epitomized everything she wanted but couldn't have.

Now that he understood her a bit better, he couldn't help feeling a twinge of sympathy for her. With that in mind, he decided to take the first step toward forming a truce.

Just before lunch, Linc headed toward her work-station to find her. He hadn't gotten any farther than the hallway outside the GRM offices when he saw Shelly coming at him.

Her brown eyes were like flashing warning signs, but he still took his chances. "Hey, I was just going to look for you—"

She stopped in front of him, arms crossed. "So you finally decided to go to the source?"

He frowned at her bitter tone. "What are you talking about?"

"You've been checking up on me, haven't you?" Her eyes narrowed, becoming thin slits, and he resisted the survival instinct to back up.

"Well, I just—"

"What exactly was your plan? Did you think turn-about was fair play? Were you looking for some way to get me ousted from GRM so I'd be out of your hair?"

Caught off guard, he didn't have time to mask his guilt.

"Yeah, that's what I thought. If you were really the hotshot astronaut everyone thinks you are, you would have put this much energy into brushing up on Draco instead of prying into my background."

Linc had been silent out of pure incredulity, but now his temper snapped. "Give me a break. I didn't hire a private investigator to follow you around and dig up dirt. I asked a few of the engineers about you. I wanted to know why you have such a giant chip on your shoulder."

"My chips and my shoulders are none of your concern. The only things you need to concern yourself with are the specifications for the spacecraft. We start training next week, and I don't want to fall behind schedule because you don't know what's going on."

Linc saw red. "I know everything I need to know about Draco."

She smirked. "Really? How many days can Draco stay in orbit?"

"Two hundred and ten," he answered effortlessly.

"That was an easy one. What are Draco's altitude control specs?"

"Nitrogen jets plus the differential firing of the main thrusters."

Linc and Shelly were so caught up in their altercation, they barely noticed that they'd drawn a small crowd. What he did finally see was the crowd quickly dispersing and Shelly staring in horror over his shoulder.

Holding his breath, Linc spun on his heel. "Colonel Murphy. Good afternoon, sir."

"I want the two of you in my office now," replied the colonel.

The long walk down the hallway to the colonel's office made Linc acutely aware of how childishly he and Shelly had been behaving. He felt like he'd just been called to the principal's office. Something about her brought out the worst in him.

Colonel Murphy followed them into the office but didn't sit at his desk. Instead, he walked to the window and ran a hand through his thick white hair.

Finally, he turned to face them, reining in his anger with noticeable effort. "Do you two know how much this mission is worth? Do you understand what's at stake here?"

"Yes, sir," they both answered in unison.

"Then why do I have two of my most valuable team members arguing loudly enough to draw a crowd when there's work to be done?"

Linc couldn't find any words to excuse his behavior, and Shelly remained silent beside him.

"Frankly, I'm stunned that the two of you can't get along," the colonel continued. "You're both well-liked by the other members of the team. You're both leaders. So if you don't have trouble getting along with anyone else, why the hell can't you get along with each other?"

Shelly leaned forward. "Actually, Colonel—"

"You know what? I don't care," Colonel Murphy said, cutting her off. "You don't have to braid each other's hair and have tea parties together. All you have to do is get the job done. You're stuck with each other. So find a way to behave civilly. If you don't work it out on your own, I'll have the two of you shoved so far down each other's throats, you'll speak with one voice. Is that clear?"

"Yes, sir," they said in unison.

"Good. Now, I don't want to hear any more commotion from the two of you, because if I have to intervene again, I guarantee you'll wish I hadn't." With that, he spun on his heel and walked out of his office.

After a moment of stunned silence, Linc and Shelly got up from their seats and hurried away in opposite directions.

Linc was still fuming on the drive home that evening. He hadn't had a problem with a woman since he'd turned twelve. He increased his pressure on the gas pedal, letting the car gain speed to match his pulse.

Whenever his father had been angry, he'd gotten on his horse and ridden until he was spent. Linc, who'd been a city boy until his father took him in at thirteen, much preferred to ride his steel horse when he was upset. His Cobra Mustang was his pride.

But that car was in the shop now, and he was driving his environmentally conscious hybrid. Though it made his conscience feel great, it wasn't doing much for his need to burn adrenaline.

Linc tightened his hands on the steering wheel, missing the sound of a revving engine and the rush of power that came with manually shifting gears.

He had to find a way to get along with Shelly—colonel's orders. He rolled his eyes. Throughout his entire career in the military, he'd never been reprimanded like that. He didn't appreciate Shelly putting him in a position to get his first reproof.

He jerked up the parking break and turned off the engine. Usually, the hour-long commute from Johnson Space Center to his ranch outside the city gave him plenty of time to work through his frustrations. But as he climbed out of the car that evening, his muscles were wound tighter than ever, and he was still muttering curses under his breath.

For once, he decided to tear a page out of his father's

book and try riding his favorite horse, Galaxy. She was black with silver dapples along the flanks that made her resemble a night sky. He'd known she was his from the second he'd laid eyes on her.

Now this had been one female he'd been able to charm out of her cantankerous demeanor, he thought as he prepared Galaxy for his ride.

He'd been warned against buying her because she'd been stubborn and extremely skittish. A steady regimen of pampering and cajoling had finally won Galaxy over. From then on, Linc thought, there wasn't a member of the fairer sex who could resist his charms.

Until Shelly.

Mounting his horse, he cantered Galaxy across his land until they were in the open, where she could run free.

Why *couldn't* he charm Shelly? She wasn't his usual type, but he could charm most women. Just thinking about her made his blood boil so much, he could barely remember what she looked like.

She was the stereotypical librarian type, who had the potential to be attractive without the glasses, pinned-up hair, and the gigantic rod up her back. But he preferred women who put some effort into their looks. He liked it when a woman wore makeup and dressed to look good for her man.

Still, no one was saying he had to date her—just get along. Maybe he just needed to turn up the wattage on his charm. An innocent compliment or two, and she'd be eating out of his hand, the way Galaxy was taking sugar cubes from his palm right now.

They'd stopped by the creek for a rest break, but as Linc saw twilight sneaking up on him, he realized he had to get back to the ranch. If he rushed, he could get in the shower before his date that night.

He was going out with Anisa, a contestant from the most recent season of *Make Me a Supermodel*, and he didn't want to show up smelling like his horse.

Shelly's stomach rumbled loudly. The three engineers sitting alongside her launched into a chorus of jibes regarding the monster growling in her belly.

"Quick! Feed the beast," Quincy said, tossing her a mini Snickers.

"What? I worked through lunch, trying to figure out a way to improve the extension of Draco's grappling arm," Shelly informed them.

"Well, that explains it then," Jason said, looking at the other two men.

Shelly scowled, shoving the candy bar into her mouth. "That explains what?"

"Shelly, you get cranky when you don't eat," Raj said. "We could hear you and Lightning arguing in the hall from in here."

Shelly rolled her eyes, trying to hide her embarrassment. She'd come to the conclusion on her own that she'd handled the situation with Commander Ripley badly from the start.

It had been an impulse that led her to ask Colonel Murphy if they could move Lieutenant Chambers up from the Beta team to the Alpha team to pilot Draco.

Dustin Chambers was the lead astronaut on Draco's backup team. If anything happened to the crew on the Alpha team—the one led by Ripley—then the Beta team would take over.

Chambers had been gung ho about the mission from the start. He had shown up for all of the briefings and demonstrations and had exhibited particular interest in Shelly's innovative designs.

He was the kind of astronaut she wanted to fly Draco.

When she'd asked Colonel Murphy the question, she'd only been half serious, knowing full well that Ripley's fame and reputation would make it difficult to push him aside.

What she hadn't counted on was Colonel Murphy telling Ripley that she'd made the casual, almost joking, inquiry. When he'd come to confront her, she couldn't allow herself to back down.

But the hallway incident had been another story. Nothing had been more embarrassing than having Colonel Murphy sit them down like two high school delinquents.

This day had gotten completely out of control. Maybe the guys were right, she thought, turning to face her engineering team. Maybe she just needed to eat.

"Don't worry, guys," she told them. "I'm leaving to go rummage up some dinner right now. I promise I'll show up well-fed Monday morning."

Raj nodded. "You should stop at Moe's. They have the best barbecue in Texas."

"He's not kidding. The sign actually says that. 'Best Barbecue in Texas.'" Quincy laughed. "I took it upon myself to investigate that claim, and I haven't found any better."

"Damn," Jason chimed in. "I wish my wife hadn't already made dinner plans. Now I'm craving Moe's."

Shelly felt her tummy rumbling, and her salivary

glands had gone into overdrive the minute they'd started talking about food.

"You all don't have to say another word. I'm sold. Barbecue it is," she declared.

When Shelly pulled into the parking lot of Moe's Barbecue, it was a quarter to eight—prime time for the Friday-night-date and family-dinner crowd. The absolute worst time to show up at a restaurant alone.

Making up her mind to do carryout, Shelly marched into the restaurant and paused awkwardly in the foyer. With a name like Moe's Barbecue, she was expecting red-checkered tablecloths and kitschy Western props adorning the walls. Although there *was* a folksy Western charm to the hardwood floors and the heavy wood and leather booths, the tables were covered in white linen and set with votive candles.

Finally, she spotted the bar in the back, and near the cash register, there was a long line of customers, which was discouraging. Before Shelly could make a break for it, a hostess appeared. "May I help you?"

Shelly bit her lip. "Actually, I was hoping to do carryout."

The blond teenager smiled at her. "Carryout is in the back, but there's already a bit of a backup. If you want faster service, you can sit at the bar."

Shelly clutched her rumbling stomach. It had heard there was a chance for immediate food, and it wasn't going to let her forget it.

"Thanks. I think I'll do that," she said, taking a menu from the hostess and making her way to the bar.

Luckily, Shelly spotted an empty seat and slipped into it just before an older man in a suit and cowboy boots could get to it.

She looked over her shoulder and smiled, and the man nodded in concession. Shelly ordered a full rack of Texas whiskey ribs and a dark beer, which she'd only recently acquired a taste for.

Despite the long carryout line, the hostess was true to her word, and Shelly's food came quickly. She ended up having a nice conversation with the shoe salesman sitting beside her. Pleasantly surprised, she discovered that dining alone on a Friday night wasn't the end of the world.

Of course, her button-down white blouse had been sacrificed to the gods of whiskey barbecue sauce, but her full belly assured her it had been worth it.

Shelly was in the middle of paying her check when she heard a voice that made the hair on the back of her neck stand on end.

"It can't be," she whispered to herself. Holding her breath, she darted a look over her shoulder. A few feet away, Lincoln Ripley was being seated with his tall, leggy date.

Quickly turning her head, Shelly thrust her credit card at the bartender. They hadn't seen her, and if she was quick, she might escape before they did.

Scribbling her name illegibly, Shelly took her receipt and headed for the door, trying to give Linc's table the widest berth possible. She kept her eyes forward, playing the "if I can't see you, you can't see me" game.

She'd only taken a couple of steps before she heard Ripley say, "Is that my favorite coworker?" It stopped her dead in her tracks.

Chapter 2

Linc couldn't believe he was seeing Shelly again so soon. If she were a ghost, she'd be haunting him.

He could have let her sneak out without mention, but when he saw her tense posture and averted gaze, he forgot all plans to charm her. Something about her absolute disdain for him made him want to push her buttons.

Colonel Murphy *had* made them promise to be professional, but this was after hours.

He could see Shelly's shoulders stiffen as she spun around to face him. With a fake smile plastered on her face, she dragged her feet over to the table where he and his date were sitting.

"Commander Ripley, what a surprise." Her tone was barely civil.

"Come on, Shelly. Now that we're going to be such

good friends, there's no need to be so formal. Call me Linc or Lightning. And this is my date, Anisa Tyler. Anisa, this is Shelly."

Shelly studied Anisa. "Weren't you on the last season of *Make Me a Supermodel*? That's one of my favorite shows."

It was odd to see Shelly smile at Anisa. Her smile was like the sun breaking through the clouds. Since she'd only given him stormy days, he hadn't known she was capable of producing sunshine. He was amazed at how much it softened her face, but the fact that she'd been withholding that softness from him set his temper off again.

While Anisa and Shelly exchanged pleasantries, Linc couldn't take his eyes off the broad reddish stain on Shelly's blouse. "I see you had some of Moe's famous barbecue sauce."

Shelly fingered the stain without looking down. "That's right. I liked it so much, I had to take some home with me."

Anisa cackled like a chicken and then started rummaging through her tiny purse. "I think I have something for that," she said, pulling out a bleach stick. "This should take that right out."

Shelly leaned over, and Anisa swabbed the stick over the stain. Right before their eyes, it started disappearing. "Will you look at that," Shelly exclaimed. "I'm going to have to get one of those."

"You can have mine. I have tons of them at home," said Anisa.

Linc watched their exchange in disbelief. Within minutes, Shelly slid into the booth next to his date. She then began plugging the number for Anisa's hair salon into her cell phone.

Anisa and Shelly were getting along great…to the point where they'd completely forgotten *his* existence.

He never would have pegged Shelly and Anisa as fast friends. They couldn't have less in common. If Anisa was a peacock, then Shelly was a brown peahen. From what he could see, in the short time they'd been around one another, she never did anything special with her hair and always wore clothes that were dull and colorless.

Of course, Anisa probably could stand to wear a little less makeup. And sometimes her clothes were so fashion-forward that Linc felt a bit embarrassed for her.

Snapping out of his reverie, Linc realized he had to get rid of Shelly before she threw his date completely off track.

"Well, Shelly, we don't want to keep you. After all, it's Friday, and you must have plans," he said.

Refusing to take the bait, Shelly leveled her eyes at him. "No, no plans. Unless you count a date with my pillow and blanket," she said, sliding out of the booth. "It was great meeting you, Anisa. Thanks for the hair salon tip. I'm going to check it out."

Linc watched Shelly walk out of the restaurant, wishing he'd let her sneak away unnoticed, after all.

True to her word, Shelly went straight to bed when she got home. But going to bed a hair before ten o'clock threw off her internal clock, and she was wide awake at five in the morning.

She'd gone to bed feeling proud and confident at

the way she'd handled her potentially uncomfortable run-in with Linc. But this morning, in the dawning light of day, she realized how she must have looked to him— like a single woman who desperately needed a bib when she dined alone on Friday nights.

It was only the fact that Shelly knew Linc already held her in fairly low regard that had allowed her to keep her composure through his teasing jabs at her appearance and empty social calendar. It was a tool she'd developed in high school, when the popular girls made fun of her lack of designer handbags and stylish clothes.

In high school she'd been a nerd, and she'd known it. There had been little point in trying to impress girls she had no chance of competing with. But in college she'd started wearing makeup, and she'd had a roommate who talked her into growing her hair long so she could teach her how to do fun things with it. Her whole life had changed then. Men had started asking her out, and she began to realize that she was an attractive woman.

She hadn't felt otherwise until now. She knew what Linc saw when he looked at her. He saw the plain, unpopular girl she'd been in high school. He had no idea that she'd learned to work with what she had. He didn't know that she'd just been too busy to put in the effort since she'd come to Houston.

Staring in her bathroom mirror, Shelly blanched when she realized that she was actually worrying over what Lincoln Ripley thought of her. Why should she care if he saw her as attractive? She certainly didn't think of *him* in that way.

Well, he *was* attractive—if you liked movie-star handsome. But that didn't mean she wanted to date him. Even if they didn't work together, they'd never get along. Two dates and they'd probably kill each other.

Running her hands through her frizzled mess, Shelly almost convinced herself that she *shouldn't* improve her image, just to spite Linc. But she quickly reminded herself that not fixing herself up for fear of what Linc might think was just as bad.

Even though it was Saturday, Shelly had planned to pull out her laptop and finish up the training procedures for Monday's session. Instead, she found herself looking up Anisa's hair salon online. It looked like a very swanky place in the photographs, and a quick click on the services page showed that their prices reflected as much.

Shelly made a very healthy salary, and truth be told, she could probably afford to pay a couple hundred dollars for her hair. But her common sense wouldn't let her do it.

Exiting to her Web browser, Shelly searched for a more sensible option. She found a reasonably priced salon that was only ten minutes from her house. And they even allowed her to make an appointment online.

After requesting an appointment for mid-morning, Shelly headed for the shower, vowing to unpack the rest of her clothes when she returned. It wouldn't hurt to have some more stylish options for work now that training was getting under way.

Miss Celia's Salon was not quite what Shelly was expecting when she arrived for her appointment later that morning. From the polished Web site and the high-tech online appointment system, Shelly was expecting the building to possess a degree of sophistication.

Unfortunately, Miss Celia's Salon had seen better days. Paint-chipped walls and torn leather chairs underscored the salon's need for a face-lift. Still, Shelly remained optimistic. It didn't matter what the shop looked like as long as Miss Celia could do some hair.

"Can I help you?" an older woman asked.

"I'm Shelly London. I'm here for my ten o'clock appointment."

"I'm Miss Celia," the older woman said, clasping Shelly's hand between both of hers. The older woman had warm dark eyes and short salt-and-pepper curls. "I know this is your first time here, but we hope it won't be your last."

Miss Celia's pleasant demeanor put Shelly at ease. The woman slipped behind the reception desk and started typing on her computer. "It looks like Tonya will be doing your hair today. Please help yourself to some coffee, and she'll be right with you."

The prospect of finally having her hair done properly put Shelly in a good mood. "I really loved your Web site. It's what convinced me to give your shop a try."

Miss Celia's face lit up. "Thank you. My grandson Troy designed it for me. He's a computer science major at the University of Houston. He swore to me it would bring in new business. Now I can sure enough tell him he was right."

After Shelly finished her coffee, Tonya escorted her back to the shampoo bowl. A young stylist, Tonya seemed nice enough as she made small talk with Shelly. And she gave her a fantastic scalp massage.

"I'm just going to put in your conditioner," Tonya said. "Then you can sit up for about ten minutes before I wash it out."

Just as Tonya started working the conditioner through Shelly's scalp, Miss Celia, who was shampooing a client two bowls over, said, "Hey, is that my Silky Tresses moisturizing conditioner?"

Shelly's eyes snapped open at Miss Celia's tone. Tonya looked at the bottle in her hand. "Yeah. I borrowed yours because mine ran out."

"What did I tell you about borrowing my supplies?" Miss Celia scolded. "Each stylist is responsible for buying her own products."

Tonya's neck swiveled as she spoke, her anger rising. "I didn't have time to buy my own supplies, because you've been overbooking my clients."

Now Miss Celia, who had seemed so sweet just moments ago, had her hands on her hips as she shouted back at Tonya. "If you can't handle the work, you know what to do."

Before Shelly could take that in, a bottle of conditioner whizzed past her face.

"Here! Take your funky conditioner. Too bad your mamma never taught you to share," screeched Tonya.

Shelly lifted her soaking-wet head out of the bowl in time to see Miss Celia duck the flying bottle. "Oh, it's on now!" shouted the older woman.

Shelly sat up, openmouthed, as the two women lunged at each other. Tonya had Miss Celia by the waist and was pushing her backward into the wall. Miss Celia reached down, grabbed a chunk of Tonya's hair and pulled.

Two more stylists rushed around the corner, and Shelly clutched her chest in relief. Finally, someone was going to break this up.

Instead, the two women stopped a safe distance away, and one said to the other, "Aw shucks, there they go again."

Shelly had seen enough. Without looking back, she stood up and headed straight for the door. Without bothering to remove her cape, she ran across the parking lot to her car, with her wet hair dripping down her back.

Spacecraft simulator maneuvers began Monday morning, and Linc made sure he was early for the pre-training briefing. He couldn't give Shelly yet another reason to question his commitment to the mission.

He showed up at a quarter to the hour, expecting Shelly to already be there or show up minutes later. He sat down on the table at the head of the room, near where she would likely sit. Propping his heel on the table so he could rest his arm on his knee, he was strategically situated to be the first thing she would see when she walked in.

The effect was lost when the rest of the team started filing in, and Shelly was still nowhere to be found. "Hey, Randy. Hi, Mitch," Linc said, exchanging hand slaps first with the copilot and then with the mission specialist on the Alpha team.

"There he is, Lightning himself," Dustin Chambers said, pausing in the doorway. "You know what they say, though, don't you? Lightning never strikes twice."

Linc resisted the urge to roll his eyes at the commander of the Beta team, the team that would take over flying Draco if something happened to his team. "It's just a nickname. Like yours. After all, just because they call you Dusty doesn't mean they think that you're old."

Dusty was ten years older than Linc's thirty-six years, and Linc always felt the two of them couldn't get along because the older man resented all that Linc had accomplished in such a short period of time.

That and the fact that if it weren't for Linc's space shuttle heroics eighteen months ago, Dusty would have been leading the Alpha team.

After Dusty, the rest of the Beta team——namely, Vince and Paul—trailed in, followed by Quincy, Jason and Raj from Shelly's engineering team.

But it wasn't until nearly twenty minutes later that Shelly finally appeared. She flew over the threshold with two overstuffed binders in her arms.

Linc looked at his watch and clucked in disappointment. "I was starting to think that I was going to have to run this meeting myself. Ms. London, I'd hate to think you weren't taking this mission seriously, as being late for the first day of training clearly shows."

Some of the other guys in the room gasped or oohed under their breath.

Shelly glared at Linc, muttering, "My alarm clock never went off." Setting her binders on the corner of the table, she pushed them until Linc was forced to slip off the edge. "I apologize for being late, team. We have a lot to cover, so let's not waste any more time."

Choking down her fluster, Shelly tried not to lose control of the briefing before it started. For the life of her, she couldn't figure out how she'd become such a total spaz since arriving in Houston. Back in D.C. everyone had respected her. Here, no matter how hard she tried to get one step ahead, she kept falling behind. Shelly was starting to think that Houston was just bad luck.

After her disaster at the hair salon, she'd been forced to wash out the sticky conditioner the hairdresser had half applied to her hair. Since it hadn't been applied evenly, it created two strangely different textures in her hair. Where the conditioner had been concentrated, her hair was extra wavy; the rest was tangled and matted.

It had taken two washings to get her hair halfway back to normal. But, as a result, she had to wear it in another gel-slicked bun. Because she'd been preoccupied with her hair all day Saturday, she'd been up late Sunday night, going over her training procedures.

She'd forgotten to set her alarm clock, and the rest was history. Linc had lain in wait, ready to mock her. But she couldn't give him the satisfaction of getting in her head.

"Okay, team. We all know that we're on a tough deadline for GRM. You all have flown on space shuttle missions in the past, and you're here because you're the best at what you do. Therefore, our training is going to focus only on the areas where Draco is different from the space shuttle. Unfortunately, there are many significant differences, and we're going to have to account for them during these sessions." Shelly looked from one astronaut to another. "Let's talk about the most significant difference. Anybody?"

Vince Patrecchio, the Beta team copilot, nodded to her. "The air launch. Draco is going to be strapped to the bottom of a B-52 aircraft and launched from forty thousand feet."

"That's right," said Shelly. "This allows us to keep this mission secret, since there won't be a high-profile rocket launch. Since we have to cram several months of training events into the next eight weeks, training has been divided into three phases. The computer simulations for launch, docking and landing, which we're starting today. Practice related to the maneuverability of Draco's extension arm will take place in the Neutral

Buoyancy Lab, and finally, we'll be doing flight testing at Edwards Air Force Base in the Mojave Desert."

Shelly walked to the blackboard and wrote out the launch simulator exercises for the day. "One difference between Draco and the space shuttle is the thrusters. So we're going to practice—"

Randy snickered next to Linc. "The last thing this team needs to practice is thrusting. Lightning definitely has that down."

Shelly gritted her teeth. Normally, she didn't have trouble getting her peers to respect her authority. But Linc had already set a tone of disrespect, and it was only natural that his team would follow suit.

Before Shelly could figure out the best way to handle Randy's remark, Dusty Chambers spoke up. "Give me a break, guys. You wouldn't say things like that if Colonel Murphy was in the room, so don't start mouthing off now. Let's show Shelly how professional we are in the air force."

"Thank you, Dusty," Shelly said gratefully.

Dusty gave her a wide smile in return. And, judging by the sudden scowl on Linc's face, he didn't appreciate his rival coming to her rescue. She knew all about the tension between them, and a sudden burst of wisdom had told her that she could use it to her advantage.

The enemy of my enemy is my friend.

Apparently, Dusty subscribed to that same philosophy. During the twenty-minute break between the briefing and the walk to the hangar where the flight simulations would take place, he fell into step beside her.

"Can I talk to you for a second?" he said.

Shelly stopped in the corridor and turned to face him. He was handsome, with spiky blond hair and a lined, weathered face from spending a lot of time outdoors. "Sure. What's on your mind, Dusty?"

"I'm just curious. Did you really try to get Lightning pulled off the mission?"

Shelly sighed. "He blew that out of proportion. It's not that I tried to get him pulled from the mission so much as I inquired if there were other astronauts that would have been a better fit."

Dusty laughed out loud. "He must have loved that."

She shrugged. "It seems Colonel Murphy is really sold on Linc as the best man for the job. Even though I don't agree, I have to respect his judgment."

"I gotta tell you, it's nice to know I'm not the only one who thinks Lightning is all hype."

"If that's what you think, why do you call him Lightning? I refuse to indulge his ego."

Dusty scoffed. "It's mocking when I say it. Sure, he had a moment. I can't take away the fact that he pulled a heroic stunt, but there's more to being an astronaut than one moment. He's getting a whole career's mileage from one good mission. Most astronauts put in years of hard work and never get one newspaper article or magazine cover. But does that make them lesser astronauts?"

Shelly nodded in agreement. "You won't get any argument from me."

"Good. It's nice to know we're on the same page," Dusty said.

Shelly turned to look after him as he walked away. *Just what had he meant by that?*

* * *

The airplane hangar had been equipped with an exact replica of Draco and all its parts. A series of training exercises had been scheduled, with first the Alpha and then the Beta team running through each maneuver.

Right away the Alpha and Beta teams took on the roles of rival sports teams, talking trash and bragging about which one would outperform the other.

Colonel Murphy was in attendance to supervise the exercises, and Shelly expected him to intervene. Instead, he told her that the military encouraged healthy competition because it would push each team to perform at its best.

While Shelly found herself secretly rooting for the Beta team, it was the Alpha team, and Linc specifically, that performed better. Dusty and Linc were clearly well-matched, but Linc was just a bit more of a risk taker, which allowed him to clock better times.

As a result, Linc was almost impossible to stomach during their lunch break. Colonel Murphy encouraged them all to eat together in the cafeteria to establish team unity.

But Shelly didn't see that happening at all. There was so much back and forth between the two teams, she didn't understand how they'd make it through the rest of the week.

Hoping to give her ears a rest so she could finish her turkey sandwich in peace, she poked Quincy in the ribs. "Change the subject. I can't take any more of this."

Quincy was a short, stocky guy with sandy-red hair and freckles. He looked at least ten years younger than his thirty-two years. He was one of the engineers who had moved out to Houston with her from D.C. Of all the engineers on her team, she was closest to him.

"Hey, Lightning, I heard you had a date with a girl from *Make Me a Supermodel*. How did it go?" said Quincy.

Shelly cringed. He would pick that topic. This was going to be a long day.

"It was great," Linc said, then dug into his bowl of chili.

Shelly studied Linc's reaction and wondered why he was reluctant to talk about his date. He'd certainly proven that he wasn't the modest type, and this was the perfect audience to listen to him brag.

"Don't tell me there's trouble in paradise," Shelly said before she could stop herself.

Linc glared at her. "There's no trouble. Anisa is a great girl."

"I know. I met her," replied Shelly. "We had a great conversation about stain remover and hair salons. What do you two talk about?"

"If they're doing a lot of talking, Lightning's doing something wrong," Randy joked.

Shelly rolled her eyes. "What was I thinking? A space jock like you doesn't want to date girls capable of stimulating *conversation*. All you're after is…stimulation. Nothing more than arm candy."

Linc shrugged. "What can I say? I've got a sweet tooth."

"Wait a minute," Mitch said. "How come Shelly has met your girl? You've never let any of us meet your dates."

"That's because he's never dated one girl long enough," Randy said, laughing. "It's been what? Three weeks already? She's only got another week or so before he moves on."

Linc scoffed. "What are you talking about? It's not like I schedule them or anything."

"Oh, you don't? Then it just works out that way," Randy said.

Linc squirmed a bit. "That's not true."

"Oh, then you're serious about this one?" Vince asked.

Linc ducked his head, with a sheepish grin on his face. "Can't get serious. Anisa is moving to Milan to model for Dolce&Gabbana on a long-term basis."

"Oh, yeah? When does she leave?" Randy asked.

Linc shrugged. "Next week."

"I rest my case," said Randy.

Shelly pursed her lips. It figured that he was the "love them and leave them" type. So far he wasn't failing to live up to her low opinion of him.

"You guys haven't considered the fact that the girls may be running away from him. After all, not many women appreciate a guy who's *lightning fast*," Shelly quipped. She heard Quincy gasp beside her.

Linc glared at her. "I've never had any complaints."

Shelly laughed. "Women don't usually bother with complaining. They just get the hell out."

Everyone at the table laughed, and Linc was visibly angry. But after a deep breath, his face relaxed. "That's okay. You all can laugh if you want to. I know jealousy when I hear it. I'm secure with my manhood. My reflexes are lightning fast when I *fly*. Enough said."

Shelly just shook her head, taking a bite of her turkey sandwich. While her mouth was full, and she couldn't retort, Linc leveled his gaze on her.

"I'm noticing that you have a keen interest in my private life," he said. "I saw you perk up when you heard there's going to be an opening in my date book. But I have to be frank with you. I just don't think it would be professional of me to encourage your crush."

Shelly's startled intake of breath was followed by a wad of turkey, which flew past her tongue and lodged solidly in her throat. Her eyes went wide, immediately starting to water as she choked. Coughing and wheezing, she pounded on her chest, trying to swallow the meat.

She couldn't hear anything but the panicked pounding of her heart as she gasped for breath. Suddenly, she was pulled to her feet, and two powerful arms encircled her. Two quick presses below her ribs and the wad of turkey flew onto the table before them.

Tears were streaming down her face, blurring her vision. All she heard were voices gasping and asking if she was all right.

The strong arms holding her upright finally released her, and she reached up to wipe her eyes. Turning to face her rescuer, she coughed out the words, "Thanks… so much."

Lincoln Ripley's face came into view. "Are you sure you're all right?" He helped her to the cafeteria bench, facing away from the anxious onlookers. "This is my fault. I shouldn't have been teasing you."

Shelly swallowed hard, taking in the fact that her worst enemy had just become her savior.

Loud enough for everyone to hear, she said, "Fine. I take it back. You'll never hear me complain about you being lightning fast ever again."

Chapter 3

Shelly kept a low profile for the remainder of the training session that day. Now Linc wasn't just a national hero; he was her personal hero. And that left her in an awkward position, given all the tension between them.

Plus, any reminder of spitting her turkey sandwich across the lunch table made her physically cringe.

Despite her personal humiliation, the incident had broken the tension between the Alpha and Beta teams. After her little quip about Lightning's reflexes, everyone at the table had shared a round of laughter.

During the afternoon training exercises, the air of competition dissipated, and the teams were rooting each other on rather than trading gibes.

Colonel Murphy certainly noted the change in atmosphere and credited it to his idea that socializing during lunch equals team bonding. He'd been right. But not for the reasons he'd expected. Lucky for Shelly's pride, no one told the colonel about the real event that had helped the team to bond.

Although the day ended without further incident, Shelly was exhausted when she finally got home that evening.

The brand-new single-level, two-bedroom house she'd bought was the brightest spot in her move to Houston. Spacious beyond her needs, it was her refuge, decorated in warm creams and tans, with accents of rich auburn and chocolate brown. Back home, all she'd been able to afford in the city was a cute but small condo.

Her living room and kitchen were completely set up, with new furniture, appliances and a few pictures to remind her of her family. But many of her personal things, like her dressy clothes and knickknacks, remained in boxes.

Shelly was just deciding between a frozen dinner or a call to Pizza Shack when her phone rang. "Hello?"

"Hey, Shelly. What's new in the world of space?" her sister Cheryl asked. Shelly's so-so mood immediately lightened at the sound of a familiar voice.

"Absolutely nothing. Unless you count my near-death experience," she said, with deliberate melodrama.

"Excuse me?"

Shelly recounted her choking incident, leaving out as many of the preceding events as possible. "Finally, someone performed the Heimlich maneuver on me, and I could breathe again."

She heard her sister gasp. "Whew! Are you okay?"

"I'm talking to you, aren't I?"

"You sound cranky about it, though. Who saved you?"

Heat crept up Shelly's neck. "No one special."

Cheryl snorted. "I know that tone. It must have been someone you don't like."

"Don't like? Why would you say that? I get along with most people," she said, stalling.

Cheryl's tone was firm. "Stop beating around the bush, and answer the question."

Shelly hated that her older sister knew her so well. But it was also what she missed most about her. It was lonely in Houston on her own.

"Fine." Shelly relented, knowing Cheryl would get to the truth eventually. "Lincoln Ripley saved me."

"Am I supposed to know who that is?"

"He's the astronaut who was featured on the cover of *People* magazine almost two years ago. It was the issue on America's most eligible bachelors, and the caption read Mr. Right Stuff, remember? You had every woman in your beauty salon drooling over him."

"Oh my God." Cheryl's voice became breathy. "You know him? He's so hot. And *he's* the one who saved you? You lucky girl!"

"Not really." Shelly sighed into the phone. "We don't get along."

"How can you not get along with a hottie like that?"

Sheepish, Shelly studied her nails. "Maybe the fact that I tried to get him kicked off the mission has something to do with it."

Cheryl was speechless for a moment. "Why on earth would you do a thing like that?"

Shelly tried to explain her run-ins with Linc over the past several days. But as she told her side of the story, she realized she wasn't coming off well.

"Wow," Cheryl said. "You're lucky he was *willing* to save you. His life would be so much easier if he'd let you choke."

"Traitor," Shelly grumbled. "I can't explain it. He just brings out the worst in me—with his smug grin and those wicked eyes, implying he can have anything he wants. He doesn't show up for meetings, and when he does, everything's a game or a joke. If I were in his position, I would appreciate—"

"That's what this is about, isn't it?"

Shelly frowned. "What are you talking about?"

"Have you ever heard yourself talk about going into space? You sound like a commercial for vacations among the stars."

Shelly didn't know what her sister was driving at, but just thinking about going into space made her giddy. "It's a sacred experience, Cheryl. Weightlessness, floating without wings. Can you imagine seeing our planet Earth with your *own* eyes? Space travel is something only an elite few get to share."

"There you go again."

"Okay, but what does that have to do with Lincoln Ripley?"

"You resent the fact that he's got everything *you* want. He's floated without wings and viewed the earth with his naked eyes."

Shelly curled her lip, immediately dismissing that idea. "I've met dozens of astronauts. Are you trying to tell me I resent all of them?"

"No, just Lincoln Ripley. He's the only one you've charged with taking this 'sacred experience' for granted."

Shelly blinked. She opened her mouth but couldn't find anything to say.

"Look, I know how much it hurts to miss out on the astronaut program again," Cheryl continued. "But there's always next time. I know you won't give up. But your dream to go into space shouldn't have anything to do with Lincoln."

"I don't think I've—"

"From what you've said, he's a hero. You can't fake that. Maybe you just *think* that he doesn't appreciate what he has. But you probably haven't taken the time to get to know him. You have a habit of forming snap judgments about people, then refusing to see them any other way."

Shelly chewed her lip. Cheryl's words were hitting too close to home. "I guess I *can* be opinionated."

"It's not your fault. You got that from Mom."

Shelly winced. She and Sylvia London were a lot alike. So much so, they'd spent the better part of Shelly's teen years not getting along.

When Shelly moved out of the house after college, things finally started turning around. Her mother loosened her controlling grip on her life and began to treat her as an adult. The two of them agreed to start over. As time passed, they continued to grow closer.

"Speaking of Mom," Cheryl continued, "have you heard from her lately?"

"You know Sylvia. Her BlackBerry has become a permanent extension of her hand. Every few days I get e-mails or text messages from her. I can't remember the last time I actually heard her voice."

Their mother was a congresswoman in Washington, D.C. She had been divorced from their father for almost twenty years and had remarried six years ago.

"And that's exactly why I don't have e-mail," Cheryl

said. "If she wants to say something to me, she has to do it over the phone. The same goes for you. Who knows if I'd ever hear from my baby sister if you didn't have to dial direct."

"You know I'd call. Unlike Mom, I actually value the human contact. Especially now that I'm by myself out here."

"I promise, once the kids are out of school, I'll hop on a plane and fly out to see you. But promise me that you'll make friends with this Lincoln Ripley, because I'm dying to meet him."

Shelly rolled her eyes. "I'll see what I can do. We've spent so much time butting heads, I don't know if we can manage anything else."

"Nonsense. You're an attractive woman. All you have to do is turn on the charm. An eligible bachelor like him won't be able to resist."

"Uh, that's unlikely." Looking over her baggy cargo pants and oversize shirt, Shelly raised a self-conscious hand to her tightly bound hair. "I've kinda let myself go."

"Let yourself go?" Cheryl sounded outraged. "What does that mean?"

"The humidity has been hell on my hair, and I haven't had time to be fashion-forward. I'm sure Linc would describe me as…frumpy."

Cheryl made a tsking sound. "I knew you'd be lost without me to do your hair every two weeks. Can't you find a good salon to hook you up?"

"That's easier said than done. All the places I've tried so far have been disasters."

"Get a recommendation. Find someone whose hair looks great and ask for the name of her stylist."

"I tried that. Do you remember Anisa from *Make Me a Supermodel?* I ran into Linc on a date with her, and she gave me the name of her salon. The place costs more than my mortgage payment."

"What else are you spending your money on? You said yourself that you haven't been doing anything but working. Splurge and get that hair back in shape. Next time you can try someplace cheaper."

"I can't believe the queen of frugal is instructing me to spend hundreds of dollars on hair care."

"Hey, hair care is my business, and I hate the thought of you walking around in front of hot astronauts looking like you belong in a homeless shelter. Buy some new clothes, too. A little makeover will make you feel better."

Shelly hung up with her sister, feeling invigorated. She didn't want to admit to herself that she cared what Linc thought about her. It was much easier to spend all her time resenting his cockiness. But after her sister's serious dose of straight talk, Shelly had to consider letting go of her grudge.

Was it possible that most of her hostile feelings toward him stemmed from her own career frustrations?

Ever since she'd been a child, she'd wanted to be an astronaut, and she'd done everything she could think of to make herself attractive to NASA. She'd attended Space Camp at sixteen, received her pilot's license at twenty-one and earned her master's in aerospace engineering by twenty-five. She'd even completed survival training with the marines after graduate school.

Yet, despite all her hard work, she'd been turned down three times in a row. That still didn't mean she was ready to give up. She would do whatever she could to get backdoor training for a space flight.

When she'd accepted the position training astronauts on Draco, she'd known she had some bargaining power. Even though military restrictions prevented her from hitching a ride into space, she'd negotiated the right to train on all the equipment and simulators for the mission.

When NASA received her next application, it would be her strongest effort. But it would also be her last. If she was rejected again, Shelly would have to face facts. Maybe she wasn't meant to become an astronaut.

Linc stepped out of the shower, rubbing his tired muscles. What had possessed him to make a date after the first day of training?

Initially, he'd wanted to spend as much time as possible with Anisa before she left for Milan. But over the past few days, his interest in her had begun to fade.

Walking into the bedroom, Linc eyed his pillows with longing. It had been a much more stressful day than he'd anticipated. Watching his nemesis choke on her food because he'd been teasing her had rattled him.

Thankfully, he'd been able to help her, but that didn't ease his guilty conscience. Hadn't he resolved to be more sensitive toward her? It had just been so difficult when she was challenging him at every turn.

On the other hand, it had forced him to raise his game. He stayed on his toes around her, and he was starting to look forward to their verbal sparring.

It had been a long time since he'd come across a woman who wasn't interested in dating him—one that might actually share some of his interests.

Linc thought about that for a moment. Why *wasn't* she interested in dating him? He was one of the most eligible bachelors in America. *People* magazine had said so.

Shaking his head to clear it, Linc reminded himself that Shelly wasn't his type, anyway. Models, actresses, women who spent time and money on their looks—they were his type.

Shelly's face came to mind. She didn't spend a lot of time on her hair; she wore glasses and had no makeup at all. But she had smooth cocoa skin that was clear and creamy, and wide, full lips that were plump for kissing, and her dark brown eyes were a pretty almond shape.

The doorbell rang, and Linc found he was still sitting on the corner of his bed, in his bath towel. Throwing on jeans and a T-shirt, he rushed to let Anisa in.

He pulled open the door, and Anisa crossed the threshold, reeking of that cloying French perfume she loved. "Just look how you're dressed. I thought you were taking me out."

Linc gave her a regretful smile. "Work did me in. Do you mind if we stay in?"

"Staying in is a great idea, sugar," she said, leaning forward to kiss him on the cheek.

Linc winced as her lip gloss left a sticky mark on his skin. He studied her face, her false eyelashes, layers of purple and green eye shadow, and shiny lips, and suddenly it all seemed like too much. He had no idea about the woman beneath those layers of makeup.

Trying to keep up his spirits, he led his date into the living room. "The problem is that we don't have any food in the house. Do you mind if we order pizza or something?"

"Pizza?" she said, curling her lip in derision. "Why don't we get my favorite French restaurant in the city to cater dinner?"

Linc gritted his teeth. He just wasn't in the mood for all that fuss. He also wasn't in the mood for rich food, an expensive bill, and the huge amount of time it would take to get a delivery to his ranch from downtown Houston.

Anisa seemed to read the look on his face. "You don't like that idea, do you?"

He gave her a sheepish nod. "I'm afraid it might be more hassle than I'm up for tonight. If you don't want pizza, how about Chinese or Mexican food?"

Her lip curled again. "How about I call some girl-friends and hit that French restaurant downtown, and you crawl into bed and get some rest?"

Linc's first heartfelt smile of the night broke out. "I think that may be for the best. I'm absolutely ex-hausted."

"I'll take a rain check," Anisa said as she headed for the door.

Linc nodded, kissing her on the cheek, even though they both knew that check would never be cashed.

Shelly noticed a significant change in her relation-ship with Linc over the course of the week. After her conversation with her sister, Shelly couldn't help feeling a bit embarrassed and ashamed of herself. On top of that, now that she'd opened her mind to seeing him without bias, she was starting to admire him.

Yes, she could now be counted among his silent groupies. Worse still, she'd started appreciating his confident but graceful strut, and the way his flight suit conformed to his leanly muscled body. She'd even caught herself studying his chiseled profile when no one was looking.

As a result of this confounding development, she avoided Linc as much as she could. She laid out the training parameters and supervised the overall exercises, but when one-on-one contact was required, she used members of her engineering team as go-betweens.

Linc made her life easy by following suit. The problem was that their mutual avoidance of each other hadn't gone unnoticed.

He sat at the back of the room when she was running briefings, he no longer publicly gibed her, and they sat at opposite ends of the table at lunch. By the end of the week, everyone seemed to have noticed the change.

"What's gotten into you and Lightning?" Quincy asked that Friday at lunch.

A slight blue tint under Quincy's eyes showed that he was tired, and his atypically rumpled shirt indicated that he was probably a bit stressed. Although those were common states for an engineer under a deadline, they never kept him from checking in on Shelly.

She shrugged. "I don't know what you mean."

"I mean, at the beginning of the week, the two of you were at each other's throats. Now you're both acting like the other has the plague. Is there something going on between you two?"

Shelly's blood rushed to her cheeks. "Why would you leap to that conclusion?" she asked, hoping he couldn't see the telltale reddening of her face. Had she suddenly become transparent? Could Quincy look right through her and see that her heart had changed toward Linc?

She'd die of embarrassment if anyone guessed how

much Lincoln Ripley was getting under her skin. She felt like her libido had betrayed her brain by falling prey to his good looks.

The humbling truth was that she was just a typical woman. One who responded to bulging biceps, chocolate-brown eyes and a sexy voice.

But in defense of her brain, he was also getting to her on a higher level. At the start of the week, she'd seen Linc as just a pretty boy who'd gotten lucky on a shuttle mission and was riding that success onto Draco. Now, at the end of one full week of training, she knew his reputation had been hard earned. Linc had smoked flight simulator records from day one. Those lightning fast reflexes—they weren't a myth. Despite her pride, she had to acknowledge, Lincoln Ripley was the real thing.

After she'd been able to let go of her resentment toward him, she'd had to admit that seeing him outperforming Dusty Chambers was giving her a thrill.

Was it arrogance if he really was *that* good?

Her new feelings were bordering on a full-blown crush, and Shelly planned to take that secret to her grave. If Linc got even the slightest hint of her feelings, she'd have to quit her job and move back to D.C. His ego trip would be complete: every woman, including Shelly London, thought he was hot stuff.

The thought made her wince, and Quincy's watchful gaze zeroed in on it. "Sorry. I didn't mean to make you cringe. I knew it was a stretch, but in my experience, when two people work so hard to avoid each other, it's because they're getting it on."

She pooh-poohed that idea immediately. "That's certainly not the case here," she said, trying not to protest too much and to control the increasing pitch of her voice.

"I know, I know." He held up a defensive hand to stall her.

Slowing her breath, she modulated her tone. "Isn't it obvious why we've been avoiding each other?" she asked. "It's because we don't get along. We're like oil and water. For the sake of this mission, it's best if we don't mix."

Quincy shook his head, letting his overlong red hair fall over his glasses. "I disagree. There's more tension between the two of you than there is between Lightning and Dusty. It's making the rest of us uncomfortable."

Her spine went rigid. "Uncomfortable? Was it better when we were bickering all the time?"

"Quite frankly, yes." He leaned close enough for Shelly to see the green in his hazel eyes. "The two of you bickering was entertaining. The two of you ignoring each other is just creepy."

"Well, I'm not sure what I can do about that," she said, with a shrug.

A smile stretched his cheeks, making his slight dappling of freckles more noticeable. "I have an idea."

Resigned, Shelly put down her ham-and-cheese sandwich. "Fine. What is it?"

"Mix."

"What?"

"He's oil. You're water. Mix." He made a stirring motion with his hands. "Look, everyone likes you, and everyone likes him. So there's no reason why you two couldn't learn to like each other, if you give yourselves the chance."

"I'm not sure that's a good idea. There's been a lot of tension between us. He thought I was out to get him. I thought he was an arrogant slacker. That may be too much baggage to overcome."

"No. Just hear me out. I've known you for years, and since we started on this project, I've gotten to know Lightning, too. You probably won't believe this, but I think the two of you have a lot in common."

"What is this, Quincy? Have you started moonlighting as a matchmaker?"

He sighed in exasperation. "I don't mean in *that* way."

"What do you want me to do, Quincy? Make him a friendship bracelet and ask him to be my best friend?"

"Just come to happy hour tonight. The astronauts are going to Boondoggles after work. Lightning said we could join them."

Shelly held her breath. "We?"

"The engineering team."

"Then you should go. I know that you live to hang with astronauts, and Boondoggles is usually crawling with them."

"You should come, too. After a couple of beers, the two of you will lighten up."

Shelly looked for a good excuse to say no, but she was secretly intrigued by the idea. "Okay, but make sure he knows I'm coming. I don't want it to be awkward because he thinks I invited myself."

"I already took care of that. I had this conversation with him first. He said I should invite you."

Why had he agreed to let Quincy invite Shelly out with them that night? Linc asked himself. Ever since he'd broken things off with Anisa, Shelly had been on his mind more and more.

She was a challenge. She didn't swoon at his feet and tell him he was the man. That had to be the reason he'd been so focused on her lately. He'd love to blame it on her being such a nuisance, but for the last few days, Shelly had made herself scarce.

Linc just wasn't used to women who were his intellectual equal. In fact, in the dark corners of his mind, he wondered if she wasn't his intellectual superior.

The closer he'd gotten to Draco's actual design and functions, the more impressed he'd become with her. She'd developed some true innovations, which could make her famous if the mission was ever declassified.

He'd never found a big brain particularly sexy, but suddenly he found himself getting a bit of a thrill when she started discussing jet propulsion and lateral maneuverability.

Her sheer enthusiasm for Draco and spaceflight made him more excited about this mission than he'd ever been before. It had been a while since he'd had to prove himself. But now he had the chance to show Shelly that he wasn't all hype. As a result, he was breaking his own reaction times with Draco.

The strangest part was that they suddenly couldn't look each other in the eye. Linc suspected that Shelly was embarrassed because he'd been the one to save her from choking.

For his part, Linc would never live it down if anyone guessed he'd gone from fighting with to crushing on Shelly. So he had to keep as safe a distance as possible.

But, according to Quincy, that only made things worse. So now, he was watching the door like a freak, waiting for Shelly to show up.

The other astronauts at the table were all from GRM. Dusty was the only one missing. He was a family man and never came to happy hour with them. That worked out fine for Linc because he got along better with the members of the Beta team when Dusty wasn't around. He'd even invited them to join his poker game that weekend.

He'd agreed to get the first round of beer for the guys. They were all regulars and had their own silver beer steins, which hung from the wooden rafters above the bar. They were each engraved with their nicknames.

He was just returning to the table with four steins when Quincy and Shelly arrived. They pulled up their chairs to the table just as Linc was passing out the drinks.

"What's the deal with the beer mugs?" Shelly asked.

"If you buy a stein, they keep it with the ones hanging above the bar. You can fill it up at a discount whenever you come back," Randy answered. "All of ours are engraved with our nicknames."

She studied Randy's stein. "Why do they call you Screwball? Because you're wacky?"

Randy laughed. "No, but the explanation is too long and dirty for your delicate ears," he said, moving on before she could question him further. "We call Mitch Brooklyn because of his accent, and you already know about Lightning."

Shelly turned to the two astronauts from the Beta team. "And what do you guys have engraved on your mugs?"

Vince held out his for her inspection. "It says Winger."

"I guess that has something to do with flying," she replied.

Vince smiled. "Actually, it's just a nickname that stuck from college. There was a band called Winger, and everyone thought I looked like the lead singer."

Shelly looked over at Paul's stein. "Gunner? I'm not even going to guess, because I'm batting zero. What does it mean?"

Paul took a long swig before answering. "I'm Gunner because I like to shoot things. Also, because I'm a weapons specialist."

"Finally, a nickname that's straightforward," she said, then frowned. "You're the mission specialist on the Beta team. Why would they select a weapons specialist for that position?"

Paul shrugged. "Weapons aren't my only field of expertise. Just ask my girlfriend, Carla."

Linc watched the conversation move around the table without him. When the waitress came by for their food order, he and Shelly still hadn't made eye contact.

"Shelly, you should get your own beer stein. But what do you want engraved on it?" Mitch asked.

She shrugged. "Probably just Shelly."

Linc finally spoke up. "No, we have to give you a nickname."

Shelly rolled her eyes. "I can just imagine what kind of nickname you'd want to give me."

He thought for a moment. "How about Shell Shocker. I certainly feel shell-shocked after going head-to-head with you."

"As flattering as that sounds," she said sarcastically, "I'm going to have to veto Shell Shocker."

Paul chimed in. "What about Tigress, Puma or Wildcat?"

She shook her head. "I'm not sure I want an animal name."

"How about Rocket Girl?" Randy suggested.

The image of Shelly in a tight leotard and cape with

the words *Rocket Girl* across her breasts brought a wicked curl to Linc's lips.

Shelly winced. "That makes me sound like some kind of lame superhero. Let's put the nicknaming contest on hold until you guys have a little less beer in your system."

The waitress returned with Shelly's and Quincy's drinks and everyone's pizza. The mood relaxed once the food came, and Shelly got along great with all the guys.

After the pizza was gone, Mitch stood up, throwing several bills on the table. "I've got to go. My kid has a soccer game tonight. I'll see you guys Saturday night."

"What's going on Saturday?" Quincy asked. It was no secret that he had a slight case of hero worship when it came to astronauts.

"Poker at Linc's place," Randy answered.

"I'm going to have to cancel," Paul said. "My girl-friend's been hounding me to take her out."

"I can't make it, either," Vince said. "My wife got us last-minute tickets to the Maroon 5 concert."

"Now there are only three of us," Linc said. "That's not much of a game."

Quincy's ears perked up. "I'll play. I'm a great poker player."

Randy laughed. "If you're that good, we don't want you to play."

"Come on," Quincy persisted. "Don't tell me a bunch of astronauts are afraid of a little competition."

"You're in, Quincy," Linc said. "Four's enough for a decent game."

"I can play, too," Shelly said. "I had a regular game with the girls back in D.C."

Linc felt his throat constrict. "Are you sure? We play for money."

"That's fine. I have money," Shelly said, getting up and heading to the bar.

Linc stood and followed Shelly. "Normally, our games are all guys. But I'm willing to make an exception this time. We could even throw in a game of strip poker," he said, just to see her reaction.

She looked at him over her shoulder. "Strip poker? Is that the only way you guys can get a girl naked? A real man would just ask."

Linc felt a sizzle of electricity between them. Were they really flirting? "Okay. So, what if I were to ask—"

She turned back to the bartender. "Then the answer would be no."

Linc watched the bartender hand her a form to fill out. She was ordering a beer stein. "Have you decided on a nickname yet?"

She turned to look at him. "I don't know. I'm thinking about Sunshine."

"Why Sunshine?"

"Because it's the perfect foil for Lightning," she said, giving him a wink.

Chapter 4

Saturday morning Linc woke up feeling more like himself. Something weird had been in the air, but now it was clearing. Had he actually convinced himself that he had a crush on Shelly London?

Clearly, he'd been working too hard. Maybe all those zero-gravity exercises had finally started to rattle his brain.

But it was nothing a little ride in his Cobra Mustang couldn't cure. Just hearing the loud roar of the engine as he sped over country roads in the early morning put things back in perspective.

Shelly was an intelligent woman, but she wasn't his type. He'd gotten past her physical appearance. In fact, he wasn't sure how he'd ever seen her as plain. Her glasses and prim topknot made her look like a librarian. A sexy librarian? The prospect definitely set his imagination to work.

No, physical attraction wasn't the problem. But they did work together. And they did fight quite a bit. He hated to admit that he was starting to like that part, too. When it came to their verbal sparring matches, he never knew which of them would come out on top, but it was fun to find out.

Still, he realized that letting something develop between the two of them offered far more complications than he wanted. But that didn't mean they had to be enemies. In fact, he was starting to believe they had a shot at becoming friends.

Returning home, Linc was feeling much more relaxed about having Shelly come to his ranch for poker. He'd figured out where she fit into his life. That had been the problem all along. Shelly had walked into his life, and he hadn't known what to do with her. Now that he could place her neatly in the friend box, without her overflowing into the romantic interest box or the adversary box. That was how he liked it.

"Adelina," Linc called, entering his kitchen, rubbing his stomach. "What goodies do you have for me this morning?"

"Lincoln," his housekeeper said, raising her cheek for his kiss, "you know I'm making two of your favorites—blueberry pancakes and spicy sausage."

"Good. I've worked up a great appetite," he said, seating himself at the counter in the large kitchen. He rarely had cause to sit at the wide dining-room table in the connecting room.

"You've already been out driving? What's on your mind, young man?"

Linc blew out his breath. The worst thing about having a housekeeper that had been with him since childhood was that she knew all his secrets. Adelina had been the closest thing to a mother he'd had since his own mother died.

She usually worked three days a week, with weekends off, but on special occasions, like today, when he was expecting company, she came in to help out.

"My Mustang was in the shop for a week. I had to give her a test-drive. Going for a long drive doesn't mean I have something on my mind," he said, hoping she'd buy that.

"Fine. I'll let you off the hook," she said, placing a heaping plate of pancakes and sausage before him. "But I want to know one thing," she added, sitting next to him, with her own plate.

Linc looked up from his breakfast, fearing he knew what was coming. "What is it?"

"When are you going to get married and give me some babies to look after?"

He smacked his forehead. "I keep telling you to abandon that hope. I'm a lifelong bachelor."

"Who is going to take care of you?" she asked, with sad eyes.

He laughed, his mouth half full. "You, of course."

She shook her head. "I'm an old lady, Lincoln. Who will take care of you when I'm gone?"

Linc stared at his plate. He hated when she talked this way.

Adelina cooked all his meals, leaving a refrigerator full of covered dishes for the days she was off. She did all the cleaning, laundry and grocery shopping. But she was so much more than a beloved employee.

She was the last living member of his family. Even though they weren't related, Adelina was his mother, grandmother, sister and best friend. He couldn't fathom the idea that one day she would be gone, too.

"Then I'll take care of myself," he clipped out, hoping to put an end to this topic of conversation. "No more talk of marriage and babies, okay? Things are fine the way they are."

He could feel her eyes boring into him. "Oh, Lincoln," she said in a sad tone. "I just want you to be happy."

By six o'clock, Linc's poker buddies had started to arrive. His official poker table had been set up in his living room, complete with green felt and slots for poker chips and cups. His refrigerator was filled with beer, and the kitchen counter was laden with Adelina's best party foods, including jalapeño poppers and mozzarella sticks.

Linc was wearing his lucky money-green T-shirt, which had faded to a dull olive but still had never failed him. Randy, Mitch and Quincy had all arrived, so when the doorbell rang for the fourth time, he knew it was Shelly.

Ready to chew her out for showing up late, Linc pulled open the front door and stared in confusion. Where was Shelly?

"Hey, sorry I'm running late. Your place is kind of hard to find," the woman said, pushing through the doorway.

He just stood slack-jawed as she continued past him, toward the guys in the living room. "Shelly?" he whispered under his breath.

It couldn't be. His gaze centered on a curvy behind in a pair of impossibly short denim shorts. His eyes trailed the smooth brown legs all the way down to white kneesocks and sneakers.

She looked over her shoulder before descending into his sunken living room. "You coming?"

Linc focused on Shelly's face and nearly dropped his beer.

This hot chick really was Shelly.

Shelly took in the dumbfounded look on Linc's face and did a private cheer.

Taking her sister's advice, she'd dropped an astronomical amount of money at the hair salon that morning, getting a fresh relaxer, auburn highlights and a sexy new haircut.

When she'd left the salon, her hair had been wound in tight, springy curls, which she knew would be way too much for a poker game. Thankfully, this time the humidity had worked to her advantage and had loosened the curls, so she could comb them into soft waves that brushed her shoulders.

She'd spent her afternoon at Vision Center, getting new contacts. It had been fun to finally put on sunglasses when she got in the car.

With just a touch of eyeliner and lip gloss, Shelly had finished off her look. But since she didn't normally wear makeup to work, she didn't want Linc to think she was trying to impress him. Therefore, she'd chosen her wardrobe very carefully. The white baby T she'd gotten from a Washington Nationals baseball game was trimmed in navy around the neck and sleeves and had a big red number eleven stretched across the chest.

She'd dug out a pair of denim shorts that she knew said casual, even if they were a bit short. Since she felt they showed a bit too much of her long legs, Shelly had completed the outfit with white kneesocks and tennis shoes.

Even though she was sporty and casual, she had to admit that the look was sexy and played to all her best features. But Linc's reaction was more than she could have hoped for. Shelly couldn't remember the last time she'd felt such a surge of feminine power. She hoped her sexy new look would distract him from his poker hand. And deep down she wanted him to see her this way.

"Hey, guys," she said, greeting them as she found her spot at the table. Then she reveled in their looks of surprise. To their credit, they recovered quickly.

"You look great, Shelly," Mitch said first.

"Great? She looks hot," Randy chimed in.

Quincy, who knew her best, just gave her a little wink. "Can I get you a beer or something, Shelly? There is a ton of great snacks in the kitchen."

"That's okay. I'll help myself," she said, jumping up again. "Where's the kitchen?"

They pointed her in the right direction, and Shelly raced down the hall and almost knocked herself out running into Linc's rock-hard chest. The collision was accompanied by the crash of two beers hitting the floor.

As she reached out to steady herself, her hands encountered a muscle wall, and she dropped them quickly. "Oops! Sorry. I was just heading to the kitchen for a drink."

"Are you okay? I was just bringing you a drink," Linc said, pointing to the two broken bottles on the floor.

Taking in the mess, she began to feel self-conscious. "I'm so sorry."

"It's not your fault. Just be careful."

Before Shelly could figure out what he was up to, Linc's broad hands circled her waist and lifted her over the broken glass. "Get us two more beers while I clean up this mess," he said.

Stunned, Shelly stumbled down the hall on shaky legs. Had he just picked her up?

Alone in the kitchen, she stuck her head in the refrigerator, taking a moment to let the air cool her flaming cheeks. Her heartbeat had kicked into high gear, but she was starting to think it had nothing to do with their little accident.

What had he been thinking, wearing such a tight T-shirt? Clearly, it had seen better days, and the soft, worn fabric clung to his muscles like a second skin.

"Are you having trouble finding beers in there?"

Shelly lifted her head out of the refrigerator and looked at Linc over her shoulder. "No, it's just that you have such a wide variety, I couldn't make up my mind," she said, pretending to peruse the brands.

"Then let me help you."

Before Shelly could move away, Linc was leaning over her, trapping her in place. If she tried to scoot forward, she'd fall into the vegetable crisper; if she tried to scoot back, she'd fall into Linc.

"Why don't you try the Fat Tire beer? It's brewed in Colorado, in the Belgian style. I think you'll like it. And I'll have the same."

Shelly grabbed the two beers, and by the time she'd straightened up, Linc had moved to the counter, filling a plate with snacks.

She handed him his beer, studying the impressive array of finger foods. She'd expected the typical bachelor spread of chips and salsa, with maybe some hot wings for protein.

Shelly bit into a chicken quesadilla. "Wow! This is delicious. Did you make all this yourself?"

Linc laughed. "No way. My housekeeper, Adelina, is responsible for all the goodies."

Shelly instantly pictured a French maid in black fishnet stockings bending over a hot stove while Linc watched. "A housekeeper, huh? Is she a live-in?" she asked, her tone clearly implying intimacy.

Linc laughed. "No, Adelina has her own home with her husband, Francisco. She has two daughters and four grandchildren, and try as I might, I haven't convinced her to leave all that and run away with me."

Shelly felt heat rising in her face again. Linc was giving her a knowing look. He'd picked up on her completely unfounded jealousy. But that wasn't just amusement on his face now.

Something was crackling in the air between them. Shelly felt a tiny bead of sweat roll down her back. Unsure of how to respond to the pent-up tension, she shoved the rest of her quesadilla into her mouth.

Thankfully, Randy stuck his head into the kitchen. "Hey, you two. Stop stuffing your faces so we can get this game started. If I'm not home before midnight, my wife will kill me."

Grabbing her beer, Shelly followed Randy out of the kitchen. Knowing Linc was behind her, she resisted the urge to tug on the hem of her shorts. Why hadn't she had the sense to wear jeans instead?

Once she was safely seated at the poker table, Shelly finally began to relax. They agreed to play Texas Hold 'Em, and that was her specialty. It took only a couple of hands for her to figure out how the guys played.

Quincy took the game the most seriously, focusing intently and taking it personally when he lost. He always pushed back his glasses and tried to look overly

sober when he had a good hand. Mitch was a more con-
servative player. He folded 90 percent of the time, so
when he bet on a pot, chances were he had a winning
hand.

Randy was the most unpredictable, because it was
clear he just wanted to play every hand, regardless of
what his cards were. Thankfully, Shelly figured this out
early, and when Randy tried to bully the pot and buy
everyone out of the hand, she stuck in, certain he was
bluffing. Her instincts paid off, and she won the biggest
pot of the night.

Even though Shelly hadn't gotten a good read on
Linc's telltale signs, it hadn't seemed to matter. He was
simply off his game, clearly distracted. She didn't dare
flatter herself that she absolutely *was* the reason, but she
was more than happy to take advantage of his absent-
minded play. As a result, Linc was constantly swearing
under his breath, claiming time after time that he'd
folded the best hand too early.

Shelly cheered when Quincy turned over the last
card on the table, completing her flush.

Linc, the only player still left in the hand, glared at
her. "Oh, you're so sure you've already won? You
haven't seen my cards yet."

"There's only one way to find out. Show 'em," she
replied.

They both slapped their cards down on the table. At
first, all Shelly saw was a sea of red, and she felt a
moment of panic. They both had flushes. Then she
heard the string of expletives falling from Linc's lips.

"Ha," she shouted. "You have a ten-high flush. Mine
is a queen high." Shelly jumped out of her seat and
started raking her chips across the table.

* * *

Linc combed his fingers over his scalp. Nothing about this evening had gone as expected. And, of course, the biggest surprise had been Shelly.

One look at her hot body in those little shorts and that tight T-shirt, and he'd never had a chance. She was constantly rubbing up against him and bending over. What was she trying to do? Torture him?

Okay, it hadn't been rubbing so much as crashing. And when she'd bent over, she'd been hunting for beer in the refrigerator.

But where were her baggy jeans and button-down shirts? The clothing she wore to work gave no hint of the curvy figure she'd been hiding.

He'd barely been able to think straight all night. Linc blew out a hard breath. It was time to cut his losses. Game play hadn't resumed, because Shelly had skittered off to the bathroom after her last windfall.

"Okay, guys," he said, slapping the table with his palm. "I think it's time to put me out of my misery. It's a quarter to eleven, all the snacks are gone, and so is the pizza we ordered two hours ago, so let's call it a night. This way Randy's wife won't have to disown him."

There were a few grumbles, but no one was putting up much of a fuss. They just started counting chips and divvying up the money. Shelly had come out on top, with Quincy a distant second. The rest of them had lost money.

A few minutes later, Shelly came out of the bathroom. "What's going on? Party's over already?"

"Yeah," Mitch said. "We have to pack up before I have to take out a second mortgage on my home."

Shelly took in the stack of cash at her seat and clapped her hands. "Wow. If I'd known that Texas Hold

'Em could provide such a lucrative supplement to my income, I would have started playing for money a lot sooner. Looks like the engineers beat the pants off the astronauts tonight."

As everyone gathered in the foyer to say their goodbyes, Linc was struck with a brilliant idea to exact a little revenge on Shelly.

"Hold on there, lady," he said, grabbing her arm as she started to file out with the guys.

She looked up at him in confusion. "What's wrong?"

"The big winner has to help clean up. House rules," Linc declared.

Shelly made a face. "Clean up? I thought I'd already done my part when I cleaned you out."

Linc shut the door and started guiding her toward the kitchen. "You wanted to be a part of my poker game. You've got to play by my rules."

She dropped her purse on a bar stool and surveyed the damage. "Hey, didn't you say you had a housekeeper?"

"Adelina doesn't come back until Monday, and she'd bust me upside the head if I left the kitchen like this for her to find."

Shelly started gathering empty plates and carrying them to the sink. "I think I'm being played for a sucker, but I'm in such a good mood, I'm going to let you get away with it."

"Hallelujah," Linc shouted, causing Shelly to jump in her tennis shoes. "I never thought I'd see the day you'd let me off the hook."

Shelly just sighed, shaking her head as she handed him plates to load into the dishwasher.

Linc took a plate from her but continued to hold it as he studied her. "You know, you've been really hard on me since day one. Does this mean you're finally going to give me a chance?"

Shelly turned back to the sink. "You give as good as you get, so please don't try to play the victim."

Linc put a platter in the dishwasher and looked back at Shelly. "You know, Quincy thinks that we should be friends."

She put another dish into his hands. "Isn't that what we're doing here?"

He shrugged. "I guess we're getting there."

They cleaned up the rest of the dishes in silence. Linc watched as Shelly rinsed the last salsa bowl and thrust it toward him.

She didn't notice the water in the bottom of the bowl, and Linc got a wet splash straight across his chest.

"Oh, no. I'm so sorry," she said, bringing both hands to her mouth in shock.

Linc shook his head. "So much for my lucky shirt. After tonight, it's becoming an oil rag for my car," he said, pulling it over his head.

He tossed it over his shoulder and onto the counter, then smoothed his hand over the damp spot on his chest. "I don't know why I ever…" Linc paused when he saw the hot look in Shelly's eyes as she studied his bare chest.

Realizing that he had caught her staring, Shelly tried to turn away. But Linc's fuse had already been ignited, and he had no intention of putting it out.

Grabbing her around the waist, he pulled her against him. Then he just held her there for a second, giving her plenty of time to adjust to his embrace or knee him in the groin, either of which was possible.

Linc's desire was ramping up fast, and when she didn't try to squirm away, he lowered his mouth to hers.

To his relief, Shelly curled her arms around his neck and kissed him back without hesitation.

Although it had taken the two of them weeks to warm up to each other, their bodies were on the fast track. The second their lips touched, Linc was nearly overwhelmed by the sudden rush of chemistry between them. If he'd known that making out with Shelly was this much fun, he would have tried to make friends a lot sooner.

He let his mouth savor her pillowy soft lips until he could no longer resist the urge to deepen the kiss. Their openmouthed kisses were pushing him over the edge. His libido hadn't been this responsive since he was eighteen years old.

Blood was rushing through his veins, leaving him a bit light-headed as he began to run his hands from her waist to her shoulders and back down again.

Shelly pulled away from his kiss, breathing heavily. "Slow down, hotshot. I'm not one of your one-night stands."

With all his blood relocating from his brain, Linc was all out of witty retorts. "I don't have one-night stands," he said simply.

Still trying to catch her breath, Shelly gripped his arms for balance. "Really? Never?"

"I don't know. I can't say never, but it's not something I make a habit of." He shook his head in exasperation. "Do you really want to talk about this now?"

Without waiting for her response, he leaned forward and slipped his tongue between her lips. She immediately melted into his arms, parting her mouth to deepen the kiss.

She began stroking his neck softly, and all coherent thought left his brain. He reveled in the feel of her palms sliding down the muscles of his back.

And then, suddenly, her hands were gone. She pulled away again, leaving him blinking in confusion at her moving lips.

"Should we be doing this? I mean we're coworkers, and it could make things even more awkward." Looking nervously around the kitchen at anything but him, she continued to ramble on. "I don't know if there's a written policy. But I'm sure the mission director would frown upon any kind of fraternization between the astronauts and the engineering staff. We shouldn't be doing this, should we?"

Linc shook his head to clear it. She'd been talking for a while, but he hadn't managed to catch any of the words.

Her eyes widened in surprise. "You *do* think we should stop?"

"No, I think *you* should stop."

"What?"

"Talking. It gets in the way of kissing." He slipped a hand behind her neck. "Unless you don't like kissing?"

"It's just that I—"

He lowered his mouth back to hers, and once again, she let her body relax.

Aware that she was feeling skittish, Linc concentrated on holding on to his control. It wasn't easy, though, because it had been a long time since his control had been this fragile.

He felt an uncharacteristic eagerness to be close to her. She smelled so good. And her body felt so delicate in his arms.

Instead of crushing her lips and plundering her mouth as he wanted, he forced his lips to trail down her jaw to the safer territory of her smooth brown neck.

Only now he was immersed in her scent, and it clouded his already hazy mind. He couldn't resist the urge to lick the indent at the base of her neck, and it immediately constricted with her gasp of pleasure.

Her hands dipped to the small of his back, just above the waistband of his jeans. Taking that as encouragement, he let his hips rock against hers, knowing she'd feel the full extent of his excitement.

Leaning into him, Shelly raised her lips to his once again. Finally, she seemed to have let go of her inhibitions and was taking the lead.

Unable to resist the temptation any longer, Linc let his fingers find the hem of her T-shirt, allowing his hands contact with smoothly muscled flesh of her back. With a mind of their own, his hands honed in on her breasts. His palms found the rigid peaks of her nipples. Then he began to pull away the cloth barrier that stood in his way.

But Shelly was pulling back again, this time backing up out of his reach. After tugging her shirt back into place, she smoothed her hands over her hair. "It's getting late. I really need to get home now."

For a second, Linc was too stunned to speak. Finally, he said, "Okay."

But Shelly had already grabbed her purse and was heading for the door. He caught up with her in the foyer.

"Do you want me to walk you to your car?"

"No thanks. I'll be fine."

He leaned forward to unlock the door, and she jumped out of reach.

He laughed. "I wasn't making a grab for you. I was just opening the door."

Shelly laughed nervously and waved as she bolted through the doorway.

Linc watched her walk down his driveway, realizing he'd gotten under her skin as much as she'd gotten under his.

He'd let her run away this time, but if she thought he was going to let her pretend that this had never happened, she had better think again.

Chapter 5

Sunday morning, Shelly was on a mission to stay busy. She bounced from one task to another, trying to keep her mind off Linc's devastating kisses.

This denial, fueled by nervous energy, was doing wonders for the state of her house. A month's worth of unpacked boxes had been emptied, and the contents put in their proper place. She'd finally taken the time to tend to the yard, which she'd had professionally landscaped upon moving in. And the dust bunnies that had been multiplying underneath her bed had been cleared away in her cleaning frenzy.

The only thing not benefiting from her busy work was her sanity. Every now and then, between dusting and gardening, Linc's face would pop into her mind. Then a flash of memory would follow, causing a shiver to run through her body.

His lips gliding over her skin. The firm grip of his hands on her waist. His dark eyes hooded with desire.

"No," she said out loud, rushing toward her over-flowing magazine rack. "I'm not going to think about that."

She'd brought a huge stack of magazines from D.C., which she'd never managed to sort through. *No time like the present*, she thought, settling herself cross-legged on the living-room floor.

Halfway through the stack, Shelly jumped in sur-prise, thinking her imagination had finally taken over and had somehow conjured up Linc's face. After her initial shock, she realized she was staring at Linc's infamous *Time* magazine cover.

She had to admit that before moving to Houston, she, too, had suffered a bit from hero worship. Eighteen months ago, he'd been the most talked-about astronaut at NASA. She'd saved the *Time* magazine cover, hoping that she'd be fortunate enough to meet him and get him to sign it one day.

My, how the world has changed, she said to herself, blowing out her breath in a heavy sigh. Not only had she met him, but she'd spent the last few weeks fighting with him at every turn. And who would have guessed that she would eventually share a steamy make-out session with him?

Cheryl would eat her heart out, Shelly thought, in-dulging in a moment of girlish pleasure.

Her eyes drifted back to Linc's face. She couldn't deny that it was a great face. It was narrow, with a strong chin. He had the perfect smile, with gleaming white teeth and just a hint of a mustache defining his upper lip.

He must have shaved it since then, she thought, absently staring into his smiling chocolate eyes.

Suddenly the phone rang, saving Shelly from mooning over Linc any further. "Hello?"

"Shelly? It's Linc. Did I catch you at a bad time?"

She shook her head in disbelief. He'd gone from her thoughts to the phone lines. She couldn't escape him no matter how hard she tried.

"Um, actually I was busy doing some long overdue housework."

"Great. Then you should thank me for saving you."

"Well, I don't have a housekeeper, unlike you, so if it's going to get done, I have to do it," she snapped.

Then she paused. She was doing it again. Did Linc somehow bring out the worst in her? It wasn't her nature to be so contrary, and yet that seemed to be the person she was becoming lately. She had to admit that she didn't like it one bit.

"There's nothing wrong with taking a break, is there? I'd like to talk to you," he replied.

Shelly's heartbeat sped up. "Now? Um, I'm not sure it's a good time," she said, looking around her now nearly spotless house. "I still have so much to do."

"Are you sure? I won't keep you long. I just think we should talk about last night."

She felt her face go hot with embarrassment. Talk about last night? She could hardly *think* about last night. Luckily, salvation came in the form of a doorbell.

"Oh, there's someone at the door," she said hastily. "I need to get it. I guess I'll see you at work tomorrow." She hung up the phone before he could protest.

Jogging to the foyer, she was so relieved to have

dodged that sticky situation, she didn't even think to check the peephole before jerking open the front door.

"Oh, no," she said at the sight of Linc standing on her front step. His cell phone was still in his hand.

As she continued to stare in disbelief, he edged past her, into the foyer. "I don't care what you say. It can't be much fun to spend an entire day cleaning."

She shut the door behind him and leaned her back against it, watching him walk into her living room. "You must be some kind of neat freak," he said, looking around. "Aside from this pile of magazines, I can't see a speck of dust or grime anywhere."

The magazines! "Uh, you haven't seen my closets," she said, rushing over to the stack of magazines, hoping to get to them before he noticed….

"What do we have here?" he asked as he lifted the *Time* magazine with his photo on the cover and held it next to his face.

"Um, I've had that a long time—"

"I can autograph this if you want me to," he said, giving her a wink.

Shelly sighed. It was no use. She couldn't avoid him. It was time to give up trying.

"Sure. Why don't you do that? I could mail it to my sister. Cheryl's a fan." She pulled a pen out of the drawer in her coffee table and handed it to him.

He scrawled his name and a brief message across the bottom of the photo. "And are you a fan?"

She shrugged. "I used to be."

"Used to be? After last night, I thought we'd finally gotten to the loving phase of our love/hate relationship."

Sinking onto her sofa, she grabbed the end of her

ponytail to twist the end between her fingers. "I have to apologize for my role in the hate phase of our relationship. I know I probably judged you unfairly regarding your dedication to Draco. But I don't think I can continue with the 'loving' part. Maybe we can settle on being friends?"

He put the magazine down on her coffee table and sat next to her. She had to resist the urge to squirm to the far end of the sofa. Now she could smell his cologne.

Again, a flood of memories from the night before assaulted her. His bare muscled chest. The feel of his surprisingly smooth skin. The slight taste of beer in his kisses.

She had to turn her head and stare at the carpet.

"I expected you to say that," he said. "But I really think it's too late for us to go backward. I've been thinking about you a lot, and I'd like to be more than friends."

Shelly felt her heart jump in her chest. Traitorous heart. As much as she wanted to resist it, an unbidden smile came to her lips at his words.

"I understand that," she said, still not daring to look at him lest she lose her train of thought. "But we have to keep in mind that we're working together. This is a very important mission for me. Probably the biggest mission of my career. I can't afford to sacrifice my reputation to have a fling."

Suddenly his fingers were on her chin, turning her face toward his. "We'll never know if this could be more if we don't give ourselves the chance to find out. And it doesn't have to interfere with work. No one has to know, if that's what you prefer."

She pulled away, shaking her head in disagreement. "Are you kidding? There's no way we could keep something like this a secret. I don't know about the astronauts, but my engineering team is a pretty gossipy bunch. Quincy is already all over me about the tension between us. He's not going to miss a clandestine relationship going on under his nose."

Linc shrugged. "Okay. Let's say he does find out. What's the big deal? We're adults. We can do what we want."

Shelly laughed. "You don't get it. You're a superstar astronaut whose stock is pretty high with NASA right now. You can have relationships with whomever you want, and no one will blink an eye. But it's a double standard for me. No one will take me seriously if they think I sleep with the astronauts on my team. I'm still trying to rise in my field. I want to *be* an astronaut one day. I can't allow anything to interfere with that."

Her last few words came out more passionately than she'd planned, and suddenly she felt completely exposed. Unshed tears came to her eyes. Feeling foolish, she got up and walked across the room, staring out the window to her backyard.

Linc remained silent, and Shelly didn't dare face him. Finally, she heard him get up, and she stiffened as he approached her back.

"You're not going to change your mind about this, are you?" he asked quietly.

She finally turned around, hoping that he understood her feelings. "It's not that I don't like you. Contrary to things I've said in the past, I've come to realize that you're a really great guy. But this just isn't the right time or place for us."

Linc sighed and finally nodded. "Can I kiss you goodbye?"

Unable to find her words, Shelly stood rooted in place as he leaned toward her. He took her face in his massive hands and tilted up her chin. Her eyes drifted shut. His lips were soft and warm on hers, and desire immediately curled in her abdomen.

He didn't deepen the kiss; he just let his lips sink into hers before pulling away.

She took a second to savor the kiss, and when she opened her eyes, he was gone. She heard the front door open and close.

One of her unshed tears trickled down her cheek.

Lucky for Shelly, the last week of simulator-based training was going by swiftly. They had a full roster of activities planned each day, which eased the tension of seeing Linc at work. They would exchange pleasantries, but there simply wasn't time for much more.

Lunchtime was their only opportunity for downtime, and Shelly handled that dilemma by eating at her desk. Not only did she get to avoid Linc, but she had plenty of time to review strategies for the following day's training. And this was exactly what she told Quincy when he asked why she was making herself scarce.

And, as a result of her effort, training was moving forward ahead of schedule. This was making her look good with the bigwigs at the National Reconnaissance Office who were overseeing GRM.

So, by Wednesday, the team had only one major simulator test left, and it involved launch separation. She arrived at Johnson Space Center early that day. During launch, Draco would be mounted upside down beneath a B-52 aircraft. The spacecraft would have to detach itself from the airplane by firing tiny explosives, called pyros.

This simulation apparatus was unique to Draco and had never been used before. She wanted to go over the details one last time, because they would be testing explosives that had to be calibrated to her exact specifications to meet her safety protocols.

Shelly entered the hangar and was surprised to find Dusty already there. She approached him, and Dusty turned suddenly in surprise.

"You snuck up on me. I didn't hear you come in," he said.

"Sorry. I didn't mean to startle you, but I have to admit, I wasn't expecting to find anyone here this early."

Dusty rocked back on his heels, a big smile spreading across his face. "This is a big deal. I've never seen an apparatus like this one. I can't wait to get on board and try it. I couldn't resist checking it out."

He stared up at the simulator in awe. A model of Draco's cockpit had been mounted, upside down, to metal panels, which represented the underside of a B-52. The body of the spacecraft was blocked out with dummy parts so the pyros could be mounted in their proper place. The entire simulator was hanging thirty feet off the ground.

Watching Dusty's face, she chuckled to herself. She'd expected the astronauts to be excited about this particular test, but Dusty had taken his zeal to a new level. He was so keyed up, he was practically jumping out of his skin.

"Yeah, I came in early to double-check everything one last time. This simulator was built according to my specs, and if it doesn't work like I'm hoping, I could end up with egg on my face."

He grinned at her wistfully. "There's no time like the

present. You want to test it, and I'd love to see this thing in action. Why don't you fire this baby up?"

Shelly shook her head, feeling skeptical. "Are you sure you're not nosing around here, trying to get a leg up on Linc? I know how competitive the two of you are."

Dusty smiled sheepishly. "I have to admit, Lightning got under my skin at first, but if you promise not to tell him this, I'll let you in on a little secret."

"What's that?"

"I hate to admit it, but the guy is actually growing on me. I thought his rep was all hype, but I can't argue with his skills."

Shelly lifted her brows in surprise. "Wow. I never thought I'd see the day…."

"I know, but I'll tell you what really won me over. Once you get past all the trash talk and jokes, you begin to see that the guy really does take this stuff seriously."

She shrugged. "Yes, but we all do. None of us can afford not to."

"That's not what I meant. I came in one weekend to show my daughter around the visitor's center, and I found Lightning in his office, and you'll never guess what he was doing."

Shelly wrinkled her brow, fearing the worst. "What? What was he doing?"

"Studying. He was really embarrassed to be caught at it. After all, he likes everyone to believe all this comes naturally for him. But he confided that he'd always felt like an underachiever in school. The only way he'd been able to overcome that had been by working harder than everyone else. It turns out that before every task, he spends hours memorizing all the specs."

Shelly gasped. "Are you serious?"

"Yeah, I know. It's hard to believe. But after that day, I've had a really hard time hating the guy."

Stunned, Shelly didn't know how to respond. It seemed the more she got to know Linc, the more reasons she found to like him. That was not helpful when she was working so hard to keep him off her mind.

Before Shelly could find anything else to say to Dusty, Quincy walked into the hangar.

"Apparently, we're not the only ones hyped up about today's test," she said.

Quincy stopped beside her. "Actually, I was looking for you." He took her arm and pulled her aside. "You've been pretty hard to corner lately, but I had a hunch you'd be here, checking out your baby."

Shelly threw her hands up. "You know me so well. What can I do for you?"

He studied her face closely. "Are you all right?"

"Of course. Why wouldn't I be?" she asked.

"Because you've been hiding. I know you keep saying you have a lot of work to do, but I know you're pushing yourself harder than necessary."

"Quincy, you know very well how important Draco is to me."

"And you know as well as I do that your newfound diligence has nothing to do with the mission." He paused to chew his lip. "We're still friends, right?"

"Of course. Never doubt that."

"Then be honest with me. Tell me what's going on with you and Lightning."

Shelly's heart rate sped up. There was a certainty in his eyes. He wasn't asking her *if* something was going on. He seemed to *know* something had gone on between them.

"Oh my God! He told you."

Quincy stared at her. "No, you just did."

Shelly wiped her hand down her face. "Oh, no. You tricked me."

"I wasn't trying to trick you. I just felt a serious vibe between the two of you during poker night, and since then, I've caught him looking at you."

She frowned. "What do you mean? He has to look at me. He has to look at everyone."

"He doesn't look at everyone the way he looks at you. And you—"

"What? I don't look at him."

"Exactly. You go out of your way not to look at him unless you have to."

Shelly sighed in misery. "Now everyone probably thinks there's something going on between us."

"No, just me. I've had a feeling for a while that it was only a matter of time. I'm sure no one else has been paying attention."

"Okay. For the record, something did happen after poker. Nothing major. Just kissing. But that's it. We've agreed not to let things go any further."

"Why not? You two clearly have a lot of chemistry."

She glared at him. "Why not? What do you mean, why not? Isn't it obvious? We work together. This is a high-profile mission. If anyone thinks we're fooling around, my reputation at NASA will be ruined."

He frowned. "Don't you think you're being a bit dramatic? I know it's not ideal, but the worst you're facing is maybe a few days of gossip and ribbing if word gets out. Beyond that, what can they do to you? I hardly think you'd be blackballed from the astronaut program."

She sighed in frustration. "You men! You just don't understand what it's like to be a woman. I'm sure it wouldn't hurt Linc's career. But I'll be known as the good-time girl. No one will take me seriously."

"Fine. Let's say you're right. Just don't tell anyone. This mission is going to last only a couple more months. Then he'll be off to his next assignment, and hopefully, you'll enter the astronaut program. It won't be an issue anymore."

Shelly shook her head, out of arguments. "It's not as simple as you make it sound."

"And it's not as complicated as *you* make it sound."

While she and Quincy stood there in a silent stalemate, Colonel Murphy walked over and started praising Shelly for how she was conducting the training sessions. By the time that conversation wound down, the rest of the team was trickling into the hangar, and it was nearly time for training to get started.

So much for her final review. It was really just her own neurosis that had motivated her to do it, anyway. The simulator had already gone through two rounds of testing and quality control.

"Relax. Everything's going to be fine," she whispered to herself.

It had to be his ego, Linc tried to convince himself as he watched Shelly talking with a group of engineers before training began.

Women didn't ordinarily reject him. That had to be the explanation for the near obsession he'd started to develop for Shelly lately.

For the past two days, Linc had hoped to find some time to pull Shelly into some secluded corner and restate his case with his kisses. If she'd let him get close to her again, he knew she wouldn't be able to resist him. How could she when he felt the same way about her?

But he'd never had the chance to make his fantasy a reality. Any time they weren't actively engaged in training events, she disappeared.

He stared at her back, with his frustration mounting. She was wearing trim navy slacks and a prim white blouse. Her hairstyle had reverted to a slicked-back topknot, but he now had a new appreciation for it. He knew what Shelly was like when she let her hair down.

Grunting under his breath, Linc tried to clear his head. It had to be the thrill of the chase. Why else would he still be so hung up on a woman who wouldn't give him the time of day?

"Snap out of it," Randy said, leaning over him and snapping his fingers right in Linc's face. "There's no time for daydreaming. Alpha team's up first."

Linc jumped to his feet, realizing the situation was worse than he'd realized. This was one of the exercises his team had been looking forward to most for weeks. And, instead of soaking up every second of it, he was sitting around, mooning over a woman.

He'd had enough of this nonsense. The best cure for what ailed him was another woman. He'd make a date for the weekend and get his mind off Shelly once and for all.

With that decision behind him, he could finally concentrate on what they were about to do.

A lift was being wheeled under the cockpit so his three-man team could climb into it. Since the cockpit was upside down, they would climb into upright seats that would rotate into an inverted position just before launch separation.

His role was to monitor the automation and take over the flight controls after the firing of the pyros. Safety brackets at the base of the B-52 mock-up would catch the simulator after a ten-foot drop and keep it from crashing to the hangar floor after separation.

Once in the cockpit, all the team members put on headsets so they could communicate with the test conductors on the ground. They also strapped themselves into the seats with seat belts and ankle straps. During mission launch, Linc would have to fly upside down for a minute, until he could maneuver Draco into an upright position.

Sitting at the controls, Linc looked back at Randy and Mitch. "Is everybody ready?"

"Ready, boss," Mitch said, and Randy let loose with a high-pitched Texas yee-haw!

Linc gave ground control the thumbs-up, and their seats began to rotate, putting them into an inverted position to prepare for separation. He listened to the chatter of the test conductors as he waited for his cue to fire the pyros.

Quincy called out, "Fire the pyros on my count. Three, two, one …"

Linc hit the button. A loud roar filled the hangar as the explosives ignited, dropping the vehicle from the B-52 mock-up. The simulator plunged several feet, then stopped as the brackets held it in place.

"Alpha team, we have separation."

Linc whooped, joined by Randy and Mitch. He could hear a similar response taking place on the ground.

Suddenly there was a loud pop and a crackling

sound. All the cheering was replaced by startled gasps. Linc couldn't make sense of all the panicked sounds coming from ground control.

Alarms started going off in the cockpit. With a flash of fear, Linc realized he could feel heat at his feet.

"We have to get out! This thing's on fire!" he yelled.

Chapter 6

Shelly dropped her clipboard and stared in horror as the simulator burned with three men inside. *Linc* was inside!

For a split second, she could barely think straight. Her entire body began to tingle, and her heart felt as if it would break through her chest. She knew she couldn't just stand there and watch her friends die, despite her knees wanting to buckle.

It was chaos on the ground. A lot of people were shouting orders, but no one could be heard above the commotion.

Quincy was the only one near her with a live mic to the cockpit, and he was staring up at the vehicle with white-faced shock.

"Quincy! Quincy," she called to him, but he just looked back at her with a dazed expression of panic. He kept repeating under his breath, "This wasn't supposed to happen."

She ripped the headset off his head and held it to her face. "Linc, can you hear me? You've got to get out of the cockpit now. The chassis is on fire, and it could break apart and fall."

"I'm working on it," Linc responded in a breathy voice.

Shelly tried to listen to the rustling over the headset to gauge what was happening, but those noises were soon replaced by static.

Seconds later the hatch on the cockpit blew out, and Shelly clutched her chest with relief. But it was short-lived, as she realized that the men were suspended twenty feet in the air and had nothing to drop onto. At the same time, fire was shooting up the base of the simulator like a runaway train.

"You and you, get over there and pull that lift back," Colonel Murphy shouted to the panicked on-lookers. "We've got to give these men something to break their fall."

But the mechanical lift had been collapsed and wheeled across the hangar to give the spectators a clear view of the training exercise.

Shelly feared that by the time they were able to wheel the lift back into place and crank it up, Draco's cockpit would be engulfed in flames. Tears clouded her eyes as she realized she might be witnessing the deaths of three friends—one of whom could have been so much more.

Suddenly two legs began to dangle out of the hatch opening. Clearly, the astronauts didn't have any intentions of waiting for rescue while their vehicle burned.

The first set of legs belonged to Randy. He was holding on to Mitch's ankles as he was being lowered toward the ground. Both men were being lowered out of the hatch by Linc.

Shelly brushed away the tears filling her eyes so she could see better. Why did Linc have to be the last man out? Once the other two men hit the ground, he'd have the farthest to fall.

Realizing what the astronauts were doing, Colonel Murphy ordered several men to get beneath the cockpit and try to catch the men or break their fall.

Before Randy could be lowered as far as possible, he lost his hold on Mitch's ankles and plummeted downward. The room cried out as he landed on the hangar floor, his legs at an awkward angle.

Now Linc leaned his body almost completely out of the cockpit, his boots strapped to something inside the vehicle.

Shelly flinched as the ear-splitting sound of wrenching metal filled the room. The safety brackets attaching the simulated spacecraft to the B-52 broke free. Now the dangling craft swung wildly to and fro, anchored only by the brackets at the back end.

The fire was spreading fastest at the head of the craft, which was now dipping precariously toward the floor. It was also where the astronauts were located.

"This can't be happening," Shelly whispered, certain Linc and Mitch's pendulous bodies would be thrown from the cockpit.

Peeking through her fingers, Shelly caught her breath. Somehow Linc had managed to maintain a firm grip on Mitch until the vehicle's pitching motions finally stabilized.

An army of hands stretched up to grab Mitch as he let go of Linc and dropped down. Unlike poor Randy, who was conscious but writhing in pain, Mitch got up and walked away from the area on his own.

Linc was the only astronaut left in the cockpit, and now smoke and flames obstructed their view of the vehicle. Shelly could hear sirens somewhere in the background, but she knew they'd never arrive in time.

The lift was being pushed under Linc's dangling body, but it was clear that he was going to fall before it could be elevated. Linc was flopping upside down from his ankle straps like a fish caught on a line.

Shelly felt her knees start to give out again. She could see black clouds of smoke pouring out of the hatch. He wasn't going to make it.

Pulling off his boots, Linc fell headfirst toward the rising lift. Like a basketball through a hoop, he plopped in. Slam dunk.

Seconds later, his head appeared over the rim of the lift. "I'm okay!" he called.

Shelly did collapse to her knees then, clapping her hands to her face. She could only think about catching her breath when firemen and paramedics flooded the hangar.

Everyone was alive. But this training exercise had almost ended in disaster.

And it was all her fault.

Training exercises for the rest of the week had been canceled. Everyone on Shelly's team had been sent home pending cleanup and investigation of the fire. Shelly had lingered as long as possible, begging Colonel Murphy and the other mission leaders to let her participate in the investigation.

She was told she would be interviewed and later informed of the outcome, but she was forced to go home with all the others.

On Thursday Shelly had no reason to get out of bed. Her career as she knew it was over. Her astronaut aspirations were futile. And worst of all, her training vehicle had nearly killed three men.

She couldn't forgive herself for that, and she didn't expect forgiveness from anyone else. The only upside to this day spent in bed, watching talk shows and sitcom reruns, was that she wouldn't have to face the accusing eyes of her team.

Around two-thirty, her doorbell started ringing. Shelly had no plans to answer it. She hadn't showered or brushed her teeth, and her hair was frizzed around her head like a lion's mane. But the ringing persisted.

Why hadn't she taken the time to pull her car into the garage? Then whoever was at the door wouldn't know she was home and would be forced to leave.

She tried turning up the TV. She tried covering her ears with pillows. But still the doorbell rang, and it was driving her crazy.

Finally, heedless of her baggy cotton pajamas and shabby appearance, she stomped to the front door. Whoever dared to cross her doorstep deserved to be frightened by the sight of her.

Her rancor immediately withered when she yanked open the door and saw Linc.

Unable to explain her sudden rush of emotion, Shelly leaped over the threshold and into his arms. She clutched him as though he were an apparition that would fade at any moment.

He held her wordlessly for several minutes and then

gently pulled back enough to look at her. Tears rolled down her cheeks.

"I'm so glad you're alive. And I'm so sorry." Her voice broke, and she sobbed into her hands.

"Hey, it's okay. You have nothing to be sorry about." Closing the door, he guided her through the foyer and eased her onto the sofa.

Sinking into the cushions, Shelly didn't lift her head. He was the last person she wanted to face. Thankfully, he was already walking away.

Seconds later he returned, stuffing a wad of toilet paper into her hands. She scrubbed at her face, realizing she probably looked that much more pitiful with toilet-paper lint dotting her cheeks.

Through her puffy eyes, she finally allowed herself to look at him. His brown eyes no longer held their wicked glint. Now they were soft with compassion. Her heart dropped. She didn't deserve his compassion.

Looking him over, she gave a little start at the sight of a big white bandage on his forearm. "Oh my God. You were injured."

He waved it off. "It's just a little burn."

Her head fell forward. "This is all my fault."

Linc's head tilted as he studied her, eyes wide. "Are you serious? None of this was your fault."

"It was my design—"

"Your design didn't cause the fire, Shelly. Something must have gone wrong with the construction or assembly. Countless people signed off on that simulator. No *one* person on the team is responsible for this accident. Everyone understands that, and absolutely no one is blaming you."

"It *is* my fault. It has to be a design flaw. I came in

early to recheck the specs, and I let myself get side-tracked. If I'd double-checked as I'd planned, I might have been able to catch something."

Linc shook his head. "You're being too hard on yourself. That simulator went through two phases of testing and quality control. You weren't the last person to touch the vehicle, so you can't be held responsible. The investigation will show that. I'm sure of it."

Shelly stared at her hands. She wanted it to be that simple. But nothing could relieve the heavy guilt weighing her down. "How is Randy?"

Linc's brow furrowed. "His right leg is broken. I was at the hospital this morning. Despite everything, he's still cracking jokes and acting as crazy as usual."

"The hospital." Shelly's head snapped up. "I should go over there."

He pulled her back down on the sofa when she started to stand. "You can visit Randy later. Unfortunately, he's going to be there for a while. Take today to get your head on straight. You're still in charge of the training for this mission. This is just a setback. These things happen in this industry. But the mission is going to go ahead as planned, and there's no one who knows Draco better than you."

As his words began to penetrate her thick mental fog, the severity of the situation became clear. Randy was out of commission. According to protocol, that meant the Beta team would now be manning Draco for GRM.

Shelly clapped her hands to her face. "Oh, no! The Alpha team is going to be shelved."

Linc winced in pain, and her stomach sank. For all the time she'd spent wishing Linc would just go away, now he really would. And now that was the last thing she wanted.

"It's okay," he said quietly. "We all know how the system works. This won't be my last top-secret mission into space, flying an experimental spacecraft, right?" His laugh was hollow.

She reached out and squeezed his hand. "This really stinks. So does this whole situation. I don't know how this happened. Since yesterday, I've done nothing but go over it in my head. Those pyros should not have been strong enough to set the entire vehicle on fire, even if it had been constructed out of matches and kindling."

He nodded. "But this is why we have training exercises. To learn from these surprises before they can happen in space. I'd much rather face that incident in an airplane hangar than forty thousand feet in the sky."

She stared at him. "The three of you could have been killed. That knowledge has to take a toll on you. Would you even *want* to get back into that vehicle now?"

He looked her in the eyes, his gaze steady and certain. "I'd do it again in a heartbeat. This is what we signed up for. It's the job. Don't you think I knew every time I climbed on board the space shuttle that I might not ever see home again? You can't let all the things that could go wrong keep you from doing what you love."

Shelly looked at Linc with new clarity. He really *was* a hero. Through and through. Like a sea captain, he was prepared to go down with his ship. Yesterday he'd made sure his crew got out first, knowing he might not have time to save himself.

All her life, Shelly had wanted to be an astronaut. Now she was wondering if she was strong enough for the job. Could she have done what Linc did yesterday?

Would she have been able to look past her fear and save her crew first?

She just didn't know the answer to that question.

Linc nudged her shoulder. "Hey, you're staring off into space. I think you're still in shock."

Her head snapped around to face him. "You must think I'm such a wuss. *I'm* in shock over all this, and *you're* the one who had to survive it."

"That's right. So, toughen up, soldier," he said, giving her a wink to show he was teasing. "Where's that hard-nosed woman who was ready to toss any slackers off *her* project, no matter who they thought they were?"

Shelly allowed herself a tiny laugh. "I guess she's still in here somewhere."

"I knew she wasn't that easy to scare off. Believe me, I've tried."

Shelly smiled at Linc, realizing that for the first time since the fire, she was beginning to feel better. The fog was lifting. Maybe the accident *wasn't* her fault.

As her heavy mood began to fade, her feminine vanity returned. Suddenly she realized she was sitting next to a flawlessly handsome hunk, and she had bed head.

She was just about to excuse herself to go freshen up when the phone rang. She'd been waiting all day for some news on the mission. Now that the time had come, she eyed the cordless on her coffee table like it was a snake about to strike.

Linc frowned at her. "Aren't you going to get that?"

She threw her hands up in surrender. "Let's hope it's good news. No turning back now." She picked up the phone. "Hello?"

"Finally! I was starting to think you'd fallen off the face of the earth," a gruff masculine voice shouted.

"Colonel Murphy?" She self-consciously looked

to Linc for support. Was the colonel calling to chew her out?

"Yes, I need you to go to Kennedy Space Center tomorrow."

Shock and relief mixed inside her. "Florida? Why?"

"To visit the launch site. Make sure they're on track at their end. We're losing a few days of training, but that doesn't mean we can afford to sit around. By the time you get back, we should be able to get training under way again."

"Okay, yes, sir."

"Call Melissa. She has all your travel arrangements."

"Yes, sir. Thank you."

Linc was watching her intently as she hung up the phone. "They're sending you to Florida?"

"Yes, to visit the launch site at Cape Canaveral. Colonel Murphy wants to keep moving forward while the training's on hold."

He stood. "Well, if you have to leave tomorrow, then I'm sure you have a lot to do."

Shelly came to her feet as well. "Um, yeah," she said, realizing that she was sorry to see him go. "Thanks for coming by to check on me. It should have been the other way around."

To her surprise, Linc pulled her into an embrace. But rather than passionate, it was comforting…and brief. Far too brief.

"Keep your chin up," he said, heading for the door.

"Thanks. I guess I'll see you…." Her words hung awkwardly in the air. She didn't know when she'd see him again.

"Around," he said, a tinge of regret in his voice. Then he closed the door behind him.

* * *

Linc climbed into his car, realizing that he hadn't let the full weight of yesterday's accident sink in. He wasn't going to be flying Draco.

He'd known this in the back of his mind, but there hadn't been time to dwell on it. He'd spent the better part of yesterday afternoon in the emergency room, getting examined.

Today his first priority had been to check on his crew members. He'd spoken to Mitch on the phone this morning. Mitch had decided to take advantage of the downtime to take his kids camping. There was nothing like a near-death experience to bring you closer to your family, Linc thought.

Then he'd gone to visit Randy in the hospital. Randy's leg was in traction, but all the pain medication had him in good spirits. Linc had a feeling Randy was headed for a dose of harsh reality once the meds wore off. Thankfully, Randy came from a big family that would rally around him.

Linc started the ignition and headed home. Mitch and Randy had their families to support them. Family was something Linc was running pretty short on.

What the hell was he going to do with his life now? Usually between missions, he'd grab a girl and fly off to some tropical locale for a couple of weeks.

But he had no desire to do that now. It was suddenly abundantly clear how isolated he'd let himself become over the last several years. Solitude wasn't a problem for astronauts. He considered his lack of ties an asset to the program.

This was the first time in a long time that he'd found

himself unexpectedly out of a job. Sure, he'd be assigned to a new mission eventually. But all the space shuttle missions had been scheduled until 2010. Then the shuttle was being taken out of commission. The Orion spacecraft, the replacement for the shuttle, wouldn't be ready for several more years.

Linc continued to brood on his drive home. Eventually, he pulled into his driveway, next to Adelina's minivan.

Maybe he could take Adelina and her family on a Caribbean cruise. Linc snorted. How pathetic was that? Trying to tag along on someone else's family vacation.

Besides, as much as he'd tried to lavish expensive gifts on Adelina over the years, she'd made it clear she wouldn't accept them. Flowers or a card on birthdays and holidays were all he could get past her. As a result, he'd resorted to grossly overpaying her.

Now Adelina's words haunted him. *Who will take care of you when I'm gone?*

He'd never placed much value on marriage and having a family. Now he was facing the very real possibility of loneliness.

Shelly's face flashed in his mind.

"Wait a minute," he said out loud as he stood in his driveway. Shelly hadn't wanted to get involved with him because they were working together.

But they weren't working together anymore. A slow smile broke across Linc's face.

She'd be going to Florida tomorrow, so he didn't have much time to waste. He had some travel arrangements to make.

Shelly rolled over in bed, and her arm collided with Linc's rock-hard chest. She opened her eyes and discovered he was naked and smiling, lying next to her on the pillow.

His dark muscled torso disappeared underneath her crisp white sheets. She reached out to pull the covers off to reveal the rest of his body. That was when her pajamas disappeared, and she was naked, too.

Before she could pull the covers all the way down, Linc grasped her upper arms and dragged her on top of him. She couldn't see what the covers hid, but she could feel it, with every naked inch of her own body.

Without words, he fused his lips to hers. Her tongue dipped into his mouth, and her nipples were crushed against his chest. He raked his fingers down her back, and she could feel a coil of heat gathering at her core.

Linc moaned her name as he pulled one of her knees up so he could fit himself inside her. Raising herself up, Shelly straddled him with her legs and prepared to ride him.

Suddenly they were both wearing cowboy hats and boots. Holding her hat to her head with one hand, she raised the other in the air and whirled an invisible lasso. Shelly bucked on top of Linc as though he were a wild bronco.

Now the bed was gone, and they were lying in an open field, surrounded by bales of hay. Feeling her desire building, Shelly knew she was close to completion. All she had to do was roll her hips….

Shelly bolted upright in bed, her heart pounding heavily. Something had startled her out of a deep sleep. Her head darting around frantically, she finally realized her telephone was ringing.

"Hello?"

"Shelly? It's Linc."

"What time is it?" she asked, trying to focus on her bedside clock without her glasses.

"It's almost ten. You weren't asleep, were you?"

"As a matter of fact, I was," she said, trying to calm her voice. She had to remind herself that he couldn't possibly know what she'd been dreaming.

"Really? Because you sound a bit out of breath."

Shelly felt a flash of heat shooting up her neck. "The phone startled me. I was in the middle of a dream. I was riding in a field. It was a Western dream."

"Well, if you ever want to ride, just let me know."

Shelly's eyes went wide. Was he psychic? Did he know that she'd been riding *him* instead of a horse? "I— I—"

"I have horses on my ranch. I could take you riding anytime you want."

"Oh, um…thanks," she said, suddenly feeling very foolish. "So why did you call?"

"I wanted to make you an offer."

Her spine stiffened. "What kind of offer?"

"Since I'm between missions until further notice, I thought I could fly you to Cape Canaveral."

"Fly me? What do you mean?"

"You know, save you the hassle of flying coach on an uncomfortable commercial plane. You can fly first class on an air force jet."

She was dumbfounded. "Are you allowed to do that?"

"Absolutely. This is official NASA business, and I have to keep up my flight hours for the astronaut program."

"I don't know. Melissa has me booked on an eleven-thirty flight. The tickets are probably nonrefundable."

"I already took care of that. She said canceling your flight is no problem. All you have to do is call her tomorrow morning and let her know your plans."

Shelly stared at the phone, unable to formulate a good response. "Um—"

"Listen. Your main argument for not giving us a try was that we were coworkers, and you didn't want to ruin your reputation. Well, now we're no longer working together. I'm just a guy who happens to be an astronaut. You don't have any more excuses."

No more excuses? He didn't know her very well. But the truth was, avoiding her feelings for him was getting exhausting. She wasn't sure she wanted to do it anymore.

"Flying me away overnight? Don't you think that's a bit forward for a first date?"

"I'm not proposing that we sneak off and spend the night locked in a hotel room—although that idea is not without merit. I just thought we could spend some time together Saturday, before we fly home. No one there knows you. You won't have to worry about gossip. And I've been to Kennedy Space Center hundreds of times. I can give you a private tour. Plus, I know all the best restaurants in the area—"

"Okay, okay…I'm sold," she said. An overnight trip didn't mean they couldn't have separate rooms. "I scheduled an eight o'clock salon appointment for tomorrow. What time can you leave?"

Linc laughed. "Unlike a commercial pilot, I'm at your beck and call. I can pick you up at your house whenever you want and drive you to the airfield. We'll be in Florida in about an hour, instead of the four hours a commercial flight would take."

"Now, that's what I call service. Okay. Meet me here at ten o'clock."

"It's a date," he said, and they said goodbye.

A date, Shelly thought. *Well, there's no turning back now.*

Shelly placed her packed overnight bag by the front door and left for her salon appointment. She just couldn't bring herself to go back to that insanely expensive salon for supermodels. While her hair had looked lovely the day it was done, the humidity had still wreaked its havoc twenty-four hours later.

If she was going to spend a mortgage payment on her hair, the hairdo should at least last more than a day. Still, she had a good feeling about this new salon.

After Linc left yesterday, she'd been in a much better mood. With a new out-of-town assignment, she'd decided to splurge on a few new outfits. The good news was that she'd found five fabulous summer dresses, which would give her a lot of choices on her overnight trip. The bad news was that her hair looked like a rat's nest.

As she'd wandered along the strip mall, Shelly had come across a lovely little boutique salon, so she'd popped in to check the place out. It was clean, colorful and modern. And, as far as she could tell, it wasn't the kind of place where any fistfights would likely break out. So, on a whim, she'd scheduled an appointment.

Now, as she walked through the double arched doors, she could see a pot of coffee in the waiting area, next to a tray of complimentary bagels and donuts. Fresh flowers sat on podiums throughout the salon, and all the staff looked professional in their colorful pink smocks with the logo for Artisan Hair on the front.

Shelly nodded to herself. She definitely had a good feeling about this place. She checked in at the front desk and then helped herself to a hazelnut coffee and half a bagel.

By the time she finished her breakfast, a lovely young woman, with impeccably styled hair, came to collect her. *So far so good*, she thought happily.

They rounded a corner, and the woman directed her to a salon chair. "Patrice will be right with you."

Shelly looked up in surprise. "Oh…you're not my stylist?"

"Oh, no. I'm Adrianne, her assistant. But you'll love Patrice. She does fantastic hair. Can I get you a magazine?"

A minute later Adrianne handed her a fashion magazine, and Shelly tried to keep her spirits up as the minutes ticked by. This didn't mean she was going to have a bad experience. After all, D.C. was filled to the brim with excellent hair salons. A big city like Houston couldn't be much different.

She'd hit enough duds that the odds of finally finding a good salon were in her favor.

Just as she was finishing an article on laser hair removal, she heard someone come up behind her. "Hi. I'm Patrice. I'm so sorry about the wait."

"Oh, that's okay," Shelly replied as her chair began to spin around. She nearly choked on her words when she came face to belly with a very pregnant young woman. "I was just read—"

"No, really, I am sorry. I hate to be late. But I swear, these days my bladder is just like a sieve. I must have to pee at least three or four times an hour."

Shelly raised her head so she could see the woman's face. She looked very young and thin as a rail, except for the basketball-shaped belly, which was stretching her pink smock to its limit. "I—I see. Um, how far along are you?"

Patrice gave her a friendly smile. "I'm nine months. My due date was Tuesday. Hopefully, it will be any day now."

Shelly swallowed hard. "Should you be here when you're so close to delivering?"

"Honey, I've got to get my paycheck for as long as I can. That's the only way this baby's going to eat. Know what I mean?"

Shelly nodded absently, trying to calm her nerves. Fortunately, Adrienne returned to give her a wonderful shampoo, which left her scalp tingling and clean.

Once she was back in Patrice's chair, she begun to relax. Plenty of women worked up until the time they went into labor. Chances were everything would be fine.

Patrice pulled out her blow-dryer and leaned in to get started. Stunned, Shelly found her cheek pressed firmly against the woman's protruding belly. Unsure how to react and unable to move away, Shelly closed her eyes and tried to ignore Patrice's belly rubbing against her face as the stylist moved around her chair.

When the blow-dryer stopped whirring, she realized Patrice was moving pretty quickly. At this rate, she'd be out of the salon at least thirty minutes early.

Patrice pulled out a flat iron and began sectioning her hair. "Shelly, do you have any kids?"

"Actually, no. I—"

"This is my second, and I've gotta tell you, this pregnancy has been much harder than the first. I don't think I've ever vomited so much in my life."

Shelly blanched. She wasn't one of those customers

that minded hairstylists who liked to chat, but she wasn't a fan of the kind who liked to share too much.

She tried hard to tune Patrice out as she chronicled her morning sickness throughout two pregnancies. Why, oh why, hadn't she brought her MP3 player? She'd always thought it rude to use them in public, but this was one time when she would have gladly made an exception.

"I was so lucky to even get pregnant this time, because my husband's practically impotent. It's not erectile dysfunction, but his sperm count is really—"

Shelly pressed her eyelids tightly shut and tried to go to a safe place. She tried mentally reciting "The Battle Hymn of the Republic," but she couldn't remember all the words. Then she tried to focus on work, but that just made her more anxious. Finally, she found an image that worked—Lincoln Ripley, naked in a field, wearing only a cowboy hat, surrounded by bales of hay.

"We've both cheated, so now we're even. And I think we've put that behind us. I've always believed if you truly love someone, you can work through anything, don't you think?"

Trying not to show her shock, Shelly simply said, "Yeah."

Thankfully, from her view in the mirror, she could see that Patrice was nearly finished with the flat iron. Just a few more sections and Shelly could run away and never come back.

Suddenly she felt a tug on her hair that was hard enough to make her yelp.

Patrice was yelping, too. "Whoa!"

Shelly frowned. "Are you all right?"

"Sorry about that. I'm fine. Just a little contraction.

Shelly's heart fell into the pit of her stomach. "A contraction! Shouldn't we get you to a hospital?"

Patrice continued doing her hair. "Nah, I was two weeks late with my last baby. These are probably just Braxton Hicks. I get those sometimes."

Blinking rapidly in alarm, Shelly gnawed her lip. She was getting a bad feeling about this.

Patrice continued to pull the flat iron through her hair. "You'll see. I probably won't have another one for quite some… Oooh!"

Shelly craned her neck to look at Patrice. "That one was pretty close to the last one. Don't you think you should—"

"Oh damn," Patrice shrieked. "I think my water just broke."

Shelly leaped out of the chair, only to feel Patrice's hands on her shoulders, forcing her back down.

"Hold on a second. I'm just about done," Patrice said, digging back into Shelly's hair.

Shelly winced as another contraction caused the stylist to yank sharply on her hair again. "But, Patrice, I'm pretty sure you're going into labor!"

Breathing heavily, Patrice continued to work. "Honey, this baby isn't coming out until I say so. And I'm not leaving here until I get paid."

Chapter 7

Twenty minutes after Shelly was due to meet Linc, she pulled into her driveway and screeched to a halt. He was waiting for her, leaning against the hood of his car.

She jumped out and ran to her front door to grab her bag. "I'm so sorry I'm late. It's a long story."

Linc just clucked his tongue at her, smiling with his eyes. "I'm going to want to hear that story eventually."

She jumped into the car, beside him. "I promise I'll tell you everything. I just need a minute to catch my breath."

Feeling anxious and a bit giddy over the unknown potential of an overnight jaunt to Florida with Linc, Shelly calmed her nerves by cranking up the radio.

Finding a local hip-hop station that was playing a popular new song, she found herself bobbing her head and singing along with the lyrics.

After a few minutes, she realized that Linc was giving

her quizzical sidelong glances. "What's the matter? Don't you like this song?"

He shrugged. "It's not that. I've just never seen this side of you."

She grinned at him. "What side? The musically gifted side?"

He snorted. "Actually, I think it's a good thing you're good at your day job, because you'd never make it as a pop star."

She feigned dismay. "What are you saying? That you don't like my singing?"

He laughed loudly. "I like watching you sing. Listening is another matter entirely."

She shrugged. "Just be glad we're not in my car. I like to listen to filthy gangsta rap. The harder the better."

He looked over in surprise. "Really? Somehow that makes sense. You can be one angry lady when you want to be."

When they arrived at the airfield, Shelly was stunned to see that they were actually going to fly in one of the air force's T-38 Talons—a training jet for astronauts and flight test engineers. Unlike the front-to-back seating typical in fighter jets, in the T-38, the instructor and student sat side by side in the cockpit.

As Shelly put on her helmet and flight suit, a ripple of excitement coursed through her. Her fingers tingled a bit when she realized that the controls would be right in front of her, within reach. "I can't believe I actually get to fly in a fighter jet."

Linc zipped his own flight suit. "That's how I roll, baby."

The only downside to having Linc fly her in the jet

was the lack of space. Thankfully, their overnight bags were compact.

"You're the first woman I've met who didn't show up for an overnight trip with at least three pieces of luggage," he observed.

Shelly giggled. "See? These are the perks of dating a girl who's low maintenance."

Instantly her cheeks began to burn from her admission that this excursion was a date. Fortunately, Linc had to turn his attention to the control panel for takeoff.

"Now that we're in the air," he said a few minutes later, "I want to see what you're made of."

Before Shelly could get out the words, "What do you mean?" the jet shot straight into the sky like a rocket.

Shelly couldn't hold back her shout of glee. Her flight training had never included acrobatics, and this was as close as she could get to the thrill of space flight.

"Do you think you can handle up to five Gs?"

"Like a pro," Shelly answered, practically vibrating with anticipation. "Do your worst."

As the jet raced through the sky, gravity began to pull her body down into the seat, and blood began rushing from her head. Remembering the anti-G maneuver she'd studied, Shelly tightened her stomach and thigh muscles, taking sharp breaths.

She held on as the plane did loops, rolls, spins and steep dives. Her stomach floated back and forth between her throat and her knees, but she'd never felt more exhilarated.

"You're a natual," Linc said. "Let's try a hammerhead."

Suddenly the plane traveled up, higher and higher, until the nose of the jet seemed to be suspended from the foot of a cloud. The air around them went still. Then they rolled smoothly to the left, then plunged straight down, pulling heavy Gs until they broke out of the dive.

"Are you okay?" he asked when they finally leveled out.

"That was fantastic," she shouted while laughing.

"You survived without losing your breakfast. I'm impressed," he said. "Now, we've got plenty of time. Tell me your long story."

"Okay, believe it or not, I was almost roped into becoming a midwife in the childbearing of my hair-stylist this morning."

She heard his voice ring in her helmet. "What!"

"Yeah, I'm not kidding. I showed up and discovered my stylist was nine months pregnant and ready to burst. She claimed she had plenty of time, and then she started having contractions while she was straightening my hair."

He looked at her again. "But your hair looked great when I picked you up. Did someone else finish it for you?"

Even though it was flattened by the helmet now, her hair had been pressed straight, with a trendy flip at the ends. "Thanks, but get this… She insisted on finishing my hair even after her water broke all over the salon floor."

Linc shook his head. "Now, I *know* you're making this up."

Shelly placed her right hand over her heart and held up her left hand. "I swear I'm not lying. I kept trying to get out of the chair so someone could get her to the hospital, but she had a death grip on my hair. I didn't think my escape was worth pulling my hair out by the roots.

"Lucky for me, she did a phenomenal job, despite wailing from her contractions every couple of minutes. As soon as she was done, the other stylist rushed her out of there. I have no idea if she made it to the hospital or if she gave birth to that baby somewhere on the freeway."

"That *is* an incredible story. You are formally excused for showing up late."

"Thank you," she said, laughing. "That was no doubt the worst of my hair salon traumas."

"What do you mean? You've had others?"

"That's for sure," she said, regaling him with her past adventures in beauty, finishing with her boxing beauticians story.

"A fistfight? Are you kidding?"

"Nope. You have no idea how much we women suffer for our looks."

Linc chuckled. "I've heard women say that before, but you're the first one I can actually agree with."

Relaxing in her seat, Shelly was surprised at how comfortable she and Linc had become with each other. It also occurred to her how little she knew about him.

Oh, she knew all about his career. He was the youngest astronaut to command a space shuttle mission. And, on his first flight in that role, the shuttle crew encountered a nearly disastrous thruster failure.

The problem wasn't discovered until the shuttle began to reenter the earth's atmosphere. One of the thrusters cut out, and Linc had to position the shuttle without it, or the spacecraft would have burned up. Many thought the task was impossible, but after a twelve-minute radio blackout period, Linc informed ground control that reentry had been successful. His lightning-quick maneuvers as he finessed the shuttle into position earned him his nickname.

Shelly studied his profile. "If I ask you a question,

do you think you could answer me honestly, without any ego or jokes?"

Linc was silent for a few seconds before he answered. "It depends on the question."

"I want to know if you were scared when the thruster gave out on the space shuttle."

He forced a harsh breath through his lips. "Shoot, that's an easy one. Hell, yes, I was scared." He looked at her with wide eyes. "Do you think I wanted to die? But there wasn't time to dwell on that. I could either give up and prepare myself for the worst, or take the long shot and try to maneuver the damn thing, anyway."

"And you did it, cementing your place in history as a hero."

Linc shook his head. "I'll be straight with you. I didn't think I could do it. In fact, I was certain that I couldn't. I wasn't thinking about being a hero. I was thinking about living to see another day."

Shelly warmed to the sincerity of his words. As she'd asked, there were no jokes or ego to get in the way. Still, that didn't mean she couldn't tease him.

"And here I was starting to believe the hype. Lightning Ripley, flawless in every way, never fails to save the day," Shelly rhymed. "And *Time* magazine agreed."

Laughing hard, Linc nodded his head. "It's all true. Every word. And if you tell anyone I said differently, I'll deny it."

When they finally landed in Florida, Shelly had just enough time to check in to her hotel room before her long day of meetings began. Melissa had booked her a room, but Linc, left to his own devices, had gone all out and booked a suite.

"What do you plan to do while I'm busy at Kennedy?" she asked before parting ways with him in the lobby.

"Actually, I'm going to head back over to the air force base and catch up with some friends. When you're finished with all your meetings, call my cell phone, and we'll have dinner."

Shelly spent a harried day at the launch site, schmoozing management, talking shop with other engineers, and fine-tuning Draco's launch protocols. All the while, she couldn't help wondering how the investigation in Houston was going. Would this all be for naught if Draco's launch design turned out to be flawed?

At the end of the day, Shelly was thrilled to finally get back to the hotel. She'd called Linc before she'd left Kennedy, and he'd said he'd already made plans for them. It embarrassed her a bit to realize how much she was looking forward to having dinner with him tonight.

Pulling her new dress out of the closet, she got ready with more care than she had in years. Had it really been that long since she'd been on a date?

Yes, it had. And with good reason.

Shelly's spaghetti-strap dress had a draped bodice that smoothed at the waist and flared into flowing chiffon. It was a brilliant white that gradually faded into a deep marine blue inches above the curling hem at her knee.

Knowing she risked going too formal, Shelly couldn't resist a loose updo, with curly tendrils falling around her ears and the nape of her neck. She finished her ensemble with dangling blue sapphires and a hint of perfume at her throat.

A few seconds before she was due to meet Linc in the lobby, she had a moment of panic. Remembering his date with Anisa at Moe's Barbecue, she suddenly wondered if he was planning to take her somewhere casual.

Grabbing her clutch purse, she headed for the elevator, feeling resolute. If he planned to take her to some burger-and-fries joint, well then, he was just going to have to make other plans.

Linc paced the lobby in his navy suit, trying not to wipe his sweaty palms on the jacket. He'd been on too many dates to count, so why on earth was he feeling so nervous?

Just then Shelly stepped off the elevator, and his breath caught in his throat. She was stunning. Her wispy dress clung to her figure in all the right places. And, even though it wasn't transparent, the fabric was filmy enough to activate his wicked imagination.

A bright smile spread across her face as she approached him. "Oh, thank goodness. I was so afraid I was going to come down and find you wearing jeans and a T-shirt."

He took her arm and leaned over, kissing her cheek. He caught her light flowery scent and had to resist the urge to lean back in for her lips.

"No way," he said, guiding her toward the doors. "This is our first date. Did you really think I was going to go cheap?"

He led her over to a black limousine, and she gasped as a chauffeur opened the door for them. "I know I wasn't expecting you to go this extravagant."

The limousine dropped the two of them off in front of a romantic bistro in Cocoa Beach. Linc requested outdoor dining, and they were escorted to a patio table that overlooked a moonlit water fountain.

Once they were seated, ordered wine, and heard the specials, Shelly looked up from her menu. "This place is lovely, and everything on the menu looks delicious. You did a great job. Thank you."

He smiled at her. "You sound surprised. Haven't your other dates spoiled you?"

She thought about that for a moment. "It's been a long time since I was in a serious relationship. So most of the dates I've been on in the last couple of years have been casual. You know, a little pizza before a movie. That kind of thing."

Linc studied her face. She looked uncomfortable with the topic. Still, that only made him more curious. He knew Shelly, the brilliant thinker; Shelly, the fighter; and he was starting to get to know Shelly, the sensual. But that left a lot of gaps in the full picture of Shelly the woman.

The waiter came, took their orders and poured them two glasses of wine. Linc let her take a few sips before returning to the topic of her dates.

"You have a pretty good sense of my romantic life. The guys at work couldn't resist teasing me about it in front of you. So, now I'd like to know about yours. Tell me about the last guy you were in a relationship with."

Shelly took another sip of wine, and shook her head. "Isn't it considered gauche to talk about ex-boyfriends on your first date?"

"I'm asking."

With a heavy sigh, she said, "Fine. We got along great. We even moved in together, but we just weren't on the same page. He wanted to get married, and I didn't."

Linc raised his eyebrows in surprise. "That's a switch. Just out of curiosity, why didn't you want to get married?"

"It's not time yet. There's still so much I want to do."

"Like?"

She averted her eyes, suddenly getting shy. "I already told you that I want to be an astronaut. In order to do that, I knew I would have to leave D.C. eventually."

"Maybe he would have come with you."

"It wasn't just about him. That's what I tried to make him understand. I can't let anything interfere with my goals right now. A serious relationship requires time and effort, and I don't want to offer anyone leftovers."

She looked over at him sheepishly. "See…I told you this wasn't the appropriate topic for a first date. I've given you the impression that I'm either just looking for a good time or too self-absorbed and career-minded to ever settle down. Neither of those things is true. It's complicated."

He smiled at her. "I understand. Believe me. I've given up a lot for my career. The difference is that society expects me to do that because I'm a man."

Her face brightened. "So, you *do* understand. Good. We're on the same page."

"Right," he said, relieved that the waiter had returned with their dinners. He'd agreed that they were on the same page, but were they really?

Linc didn't know when or how it had happened, but his priorities had shifted. His ranch was pretty empty most of the time, and he used to revel in the solitude. Now he was starting to like the thought of seeing the same face every day when he came home.

When he landed at the end of a mission, all his crew members had spouses and children waiting to greet them. He rarely had anyone. When he did, it was never the same woman twice. Now he wanted that to change.

Even if he *was* ready to settle down with someone, that certainly didn't mean that someone had to be Shelly. But she was the one who'd started him thinking along those lines.

She hadn't needed to remind him that she was more than just a good-time girl. She demanded too much respect for any man to place her in that category.

And she wouldn't be some shrinking violet who would become a domestic slave. No, she would be a challenge to her future husband—always expressing her thoughts and ideas. She was so passionate about everything, and that would carry over to the bedroom. Then before long, she'd be pregnant….

A slow smile spread across his face.

"What are you grinning about?" Shelly asked. "You seem to have drifted off somewhere. What's on your mind?"

Linc focused on her pretty face. It was long and narrow, emphasizing her lush plum lips. With her soft brown curls piled up on her head, he could see her long neck. And her wide, expressive eyes were now focused intently on him.

"One day I'll tell you. But not now."

She eyed him suspiciously. "What is it? Is there spinach in my teeth or something?"

"No, nothing like that. Just relax and enjoy the moment."

Their intimate conversation at the start of the meal had broken the ice, creating a much more relaxed atmosphere for the rest of dinner. The food was excellent, and they laughed and joked right through to dessert.

On the limousine ride back to the hotel, Linc took the opportunity to get closer to Shelly, the way he'd wanted to all night.

"Why are you sitting so far away? Don't be a stranger," he said, sliding next to her.

"I was keeping my distance because I recognize that dangerous look in your eyes."

"Oh, yeah? And what's that look I see in your eyes?"

She rose up on one knee, and within seconds she was straddling him. "I'm pretty dangerous, too."

Linc didn't have time to register his surprise. Her lips were already coming down over his. His body instantly reacted, and from the position of their bodies, she couldn't miss it.

"Ahh, you're a rocket man," she whispered in his ear.

He wanted to laugh, but he didn't have enough breath. Her tongue was making slow spirals around the outer rim of his ear, while her fingers stroked his head and neck.

His hands slipped under her dress and up her long, sleek thighs. He tucked his thumb under the edge of her lacy bikini panties.

One quick tug and he could be inside her. He hooked his fingers around both sides of her panties and began to pull them down.

"Whoa," Shelly said breathlessly. "This is getting out of control."

A sudden whirring noise froze them in place. The privacy screen was lowering. Flustered, the chauffeur stammered, "Sorry... Uh, I need to see out of the back window. Traffic. There's traffic."

Shelly and Linc leaped to their opposite corners. Even though the screen slid back into place a few minutes later, neither of them moved again.

Back at the hotel, Linc got off the elevator on Shelly's floor. As she pulled out her door key, he leaned over her.

"Can I come in?" he asked.

She faced him, leaning her back against the door, and said, simply, "No."

Undaunted, Linc said, "Then come up to my room. It's a suite. King-size bed. Plenty of room for the two of us."

Shelly wagged her finger at him. "Ah, ah, ah, you promised to behave like a gentleman."

After letting a swear word unbecoming a gentleman fly from his lips, he grumbled, "What in hell possessed me to promise a foolish thing like that?"

"Good night, Linc," she said firmly.

Linc took Shelly gently by the neck and slipped his tongue into her mouth. He kissed her forcefully, as if to leave his imprint on her. He moved his lips back and forth across hers, until he felt her knees start to shake.

Satisfied, he stepped away. "I'll see you tomorrow."

Shelly just nodded, staring after him. When he looked back, she was still standing there.

"What am I going to do?" Shelly asked her mirrored reflection before she was due to meet up with Linc the next morning.

After their romantic dinner, their steamy limo ride and that knee-buckling kiss at the door, she had to face the miserable truth.

He had her.

She wanted him. She wanted him so badly that if he knocked on the door right then and said, "Let's do this," she wouldn't be able to say no.

How could she? He was the total package. Movie-star face, mouthwatering body, and he was Mensa smart, with a heroic reputation as an astronaut.

These were all the things she'd loved to hate about him from the start, and now she, too, had fallen into the trap.

Now Shelly had the very real fear that she would be completely at the mercy of his mojo. Before long, he'd have her standing on one leg and barking like a dog. She hated the idea of wanting a man that much. That had to be why she'd never allowed herself to do so.

And, despite all her big talk at dinner the night before, if she did let Linc get under her skin, she'd be devastated if he inevitably got tired of her.

Her cell phone rang, and it was him. "Shelly, I'm waiting in the lobby. Where are you?"

This was her chance. She could tell him that she was sick and that she needed to go home right away. She didn't have to stay caught in his web.

But it was no use. She wanted to spend the day with Linc. She was looking forward to it. And even though she was driving down an unlit road that could possibly lead off a cliff, there was no turning back now.

"I'll be right down."

It had been a fun day. In fact, Linc couldn't remember the last time he'd had that much fun on a date. Shelly didn't need him to prove his affection with his wallet, and she didn't require that they hang out in venues where they could see and be seen. It had been a refreshing change.

Shelly hadn't minded kicking off her shoes and getting her feet caked with wet sand at the Cocoa Beach Pier. She'd actually laughed when she got ketchup on her nose when they'd shared some fries at lunch. And, there had been no constant compact checks or lipstick touch-ups throughout the day. Instead, she'd been entirely focused on him, and that had felt good.

He'd been staring at the manufactured faces of models and the like for so long that he hadn't been able to appreciate Shelly's natural beauty at first.

Now she was the most beautiful woman he'd ever seen. Long lashes without glue and full lips without collagen. She had flawless brown skin, and he could actually touch it without getting makeup on his fingers. And her figure…her full breasts and hips, and those…

Well, he couldn't think about that now, or he'd crash the plane. They were thirty thousand feet in the air, and they still had a way to go.

Linc had to get his mind on something else. "Can I ask you a question, Shelly?"

Apparently, she'd been about to doze off, and she jerked in her seat. "Huh? A question? Sure."

"I know you want to be an astronaut, but have you applied to the program yet?"

Shelly remained silent, and when Linc looked over at her, he could see that she was actually blushing.

"What is it?" he asked.

Clearly embarrassed, she finally said, "I applied three times."

That caught Linc off guard. And as her words sank in, he began to understand her initial bitterness toward him much better. She'd always viewed him as taking everything about GRM so lightly. Knowing how long she'd been struggling to get where he was, he couldn't blame her for resenting him.

Trying not to embarrass her further, Linc gently broached the subject again. "It's a very competitive program. Maybe if you tell me about your qualifications, I can give you some advice on what to work on." Linc held his breath, half expecting her to become defensive.

"Okay. I'll take whatever help I can get."

"Great," Linc said in surprise and relief. "Go ahead."

"Um, where do I start? I've wanted to be an astronaut since I was a kid. When I was sixteen, I begged my mother to send me to Space Camp. From then on, I focused on anything that might make me a stronger candidate for astronaut training."

Linc listened in awe as Shelly listed her advanced degree in aerospace engineering, her week doing survival training with the marines and running the obstacle course at Quantico.

"I even got my pilot's license when I was twenty-one, because I thought that would clinch the deal."

"I didn't know you could fly, Shelly."

She just shrugged, still focused on the topic at hand. "With my first application, I made it to the weeklong interview process. I thought it went really well. I passed the physical, so I thought I had a good chance. But that was the end of it. My next two applications never even got *that* far."

Linc wrinkled his nose. "I'm surprised you didn't at least get into the training program. You're a woman and a minority and more qualified than half the candidates that were in my astronaut class."

Shelly sighed. "I recently sent in one last application. If I don't make it this time, there's nothing I can do. As part of my contract when I came here for GRM, I made NASA agree to allow me to train on all the equipment myself. I told them that it was to allow me to be a better trainer. But I'm really hoping the program will view it as field experience."

Linc shook his head, suspicious. He'd based his career on his instincts, and they were telling him that something just wasn't right. Shelly was the epitome of what the program looked for in astronaut candidates. She had the academic background and met all the physical requirements, in addition to her bonus experiences, like Space Camp, marine training, and flight hours, which should have made her almost irresistible.

Maybe this was something he could look into. But he wouldn't tell her his suspicions yet, just in case his hunch proved false.

Instead, he needed to pull her out of the brooding mood his questions had put her in. "Hey, Shelly, do you want to fly the plane?"

"Are you kidding me? Hell, yes," she said, eagerly taking over the controls in front of her.

It was dark when Linc finally dropped Shelly off at home. Placing her overnight bag in front of her door, he shifted from foot to foot. All he wanted was for her to invite him in.

With her key in the door, she looked over her shoulder. "Thanks for letting me fly. I had a great time. You made a mundane business trip so much fun."

"I aim to serve," he answered, resisting the urge to ask if he could stay the night. It had taken so long for their relationship to progress to this point. Instinct told him that if he tried to push, she'd back off again.

His hopes leaped when she stepped up to him and raised her face for a kiss. He let her set the tone. He felt the soft brush of her lips before she moved away. "I guess we'll be in touch?"

"I guess so," he replied, hiding his disappointment as he walked back to his car.

Chapter 8

Sunday was a restless day for Shelly. She didn't feel like cleaning, and she didn't feel like watching television. All she wanted to do was review the huge mistake she'd made last night.

Why hadn't she invited Linc to stay the night? She'd been such a coward. It had been on her mind all day, and when it had come time for her to say the words, they just wouldn't come.

She'd been scared.

Sleeping with Linc would change everything. No more denial. No room to pretend she could take him or leave him like a bowl of vanilla swirl ice cream.

When the phone rang around noon, Shelly found herself running to it like a lunatic. It had to be Linc. "Hello?"

"Shelly, it's Colonel Murphy."

Her heart sank. Strangely enough, her first concern was that it *wasn't* Linc. Her second thought was that the investigation must be over.

"Yesterday evening the National Reconnaissance Office concluded that the fire on Draco's simulator was caused by the pyros. Your specifications called for smaller charges than the ones that were used."

Shelly's brows knit. The simulator had been through several rounds of inspection before testing. Someone would have caught an installation error. "Are you saying someone tampered with the pyros?"

"It's a possibility. That portion of the investigation is still ongoing. We know your design specifications were accurate."

Shelly couldn't help feeling a deep sense of relief.

"In any case," he continued, "there's going to have to be some overlap in the investigation and our moving ahead with training. The only thing we can do to bridge the gap is increase security. The contractors are working around the clock to install a badge-recognition security system on all the rooms that house GRM equipment. Every event will be assigned a security level, and only the most essential personnel will be granted access. Now, if incidents like this one occur in the future, there will be a finite list of suspects."

"When do you expect training to resume?"

"We should be finished with all the repairs and security upgrades by midweek. Until then, I want you to focus on any areas where time can be trimmed off the training schedule."

Shelly assured Colonel Murphy that she'd do whatever she could, and hung up the phone, with her mind reeling.

Sabotage? How could that be possible? GRM was classified top-secret, which meant fewer people than usual even knew what it was. Why would anyone want to see it derailed?

Before she could dwell on the matter further, her phone rang again. "Hello," she said, answering it, still preoccupied.

Linc's voice came over the line. "Shelly, I wanted to invite you—"

"You're never going to believe what Colonel Murphy just told me." As the words were leaving her mouth, she paused. Linc was off GRM. Would it be a breach of security to tell him what she'd learned?

"What is it? Tell me."

Linc had risked his life on that simulator. There was no way he could be responsible for the fire, she rationalized. "The simulator fire may have been deliberate. The pyros on the vehicle were replaced with larger explosives than the specs stipulated."

Linc sucked in his breath in shock. "I can't believe it."

"Me neither. I can't imagine who could be responsible."

Linc was quiet for a moment. "I shouldn't be speculating out loud, but I just had a scary thought."

Shelly's ears perked up. "What is it?"

"What if it was Dusty Chambers?"

"Dusty," she said, staring at the phone as if he'd just suggested Santa Claus. "Why on earth would he do something like that? I know there's been a lot of tension between the two of you, but Dusty's an astronaut."

"Think about it. Who had the most to gain when the Alpha team was put out of commission? Dusty. His team is now the lead on GRM."

Shelly still wasn't buying it. "I don't know, Linc. His team was supposed to get in that simulator, too. What if the order had been switched and the Beta team had had to test the simulator first?"

"The Alpha team always goes first," he said adamantly. "And, didn't I see you talking to him before training began that day? Was he asking a lot of questions or showing extra interest in how things work?"

Shelly paused, thinking back to that morning. "I showed up early to check the specs, and Dusty was the main reason I got sidetracked. He was in the hangar before I even got there. Dusty *was* fascinated with the test, but that doesn't mean—"

"Interesting. So, if he knew what he was doing, he could have been the one to tamper with the pyros."

"But how could Dusty know enough about the technology to change it?" she asked. "There had to be forty or fifty people in the hangar at the time of the accident. And even more people at Johnson had access to that hangar."

"I'm not saying it's conclusive. I'm just saying it had to be some kind of inside job, and he and his team had the most to gain. The fact that you found him in the hangar so early doesn't help his case."

Shelly sighed in exasperation. "But he's an astronaut."

"And? Shelly, you have stars in your eyes when it comes to the noble astronaut. They're just as capable of wrongdoing as anyone else."

"You don't understand. Dusty and I were talking about you that morning. He told me how much he'd come to admire your professionalism. He said he was starting to like you."

"Isn't that convenient? He made sure someone heard

him singing my praises before I nearly died in that simulator fire."

She shook her head in resignation. She would never be able to believe that Dusty or any of the astronauts were capable of such things. But someone *had* changed the pyros. Shelly thought back to her talk with Dusty on the first day of training. Prior to the launch separation test, he *had* been very negative toward Linc.

"Do you plan to tell Colonel Murphy about your suspicions?"

"Of course. Even though I don't have any hard evidence, I'm sure every theory is welcome," Linc replied.

Shelly chewed her lip in worry. "What if they ultimately decide to abort this mission?"

"Trust me, Shelly. You haven't learned this yet, but you will. NASA always has a backup plan." While she let that sink in, Linc asked, "When do they think training will resume?"

"Not until midweek. They're setting up a slew of new security measures."

Linc was quiet for a moment. "Since training won't resume for a few more days, why don't you spend your downtime at my ranch?"

Shelly's heart began to hammer with anticipation. "Your ranch?"

"Yes, it will be relaxing for you, and we can ride horses, swim…make love. I think you should say yes."

Her brain was stuck on *make love*. Her mind drifted back to her sexy dream a few days earlier. "Does your ranch have a field and bales of hay?"

"Uh, yeah, I guess," he answered, sounding completely puzzled by her question.

"Okay. I'm in."

* * *

Trying to tamp down his overflowing anticipation, Linc sat in his den and pretended to watch the golf channel.

But, in reality, he had no hope of concentrating. He'd thrown an offer out on the table, and by accepting his invitation to visit his ranch, she'd agreed to it.

Everything was set. Not wanting to feed Shelly Adelina's delicious but frozen premade meals, he got takeout from his favorite Mexican restaurant. The table was set for romance, and the food was warming in the oven.

Now, all he had to do was maintain his composure long enough to get through dinner without jumping her. The problem was that he'd been celibate since he'd started having feelings for Shelly, and he wasn't at all sure he was up to the challenge of restraining himself.

When the doorbell finally rang, Linc's heart started banging so hard, he was sure it could be heard outside his chest. He pulled open the door, and his stomach dropped to his feet. Blood rushed to his groin, and any hope of restraint evaporated.

She walked into the foyer, rolling her travel bag behind her. She was dressed in skintight dark denim jeans, and she'd knotted a red-checked button-down shirt just under her breasts. Her flat brown stomach and her lush cleavage were exposed. Finishing the look, she'd braided her hair into pigtails on either side of her head.

"What do you think?" she asked. "I figured if I was going to spend some time on a ranch, I should look the part."

Linc's brain had already shut down, and he had no words to answer her. With an animalistic grunt, he reacted on instinct. Grabbing her around her bared waist, he lifted her against him, and she was forced to wrap her legs around him.

She released a guttural sound of pleasure just as her mouth crushed his. Her soft lips were already parting for him to enter her.

Fully erect and quickly losing control, Linc rocked their pelvises together. Needing more support, he carried her a few steps and pressed her back against the wall. Now he had the leverage to hold her in place as he locked her hands above her head with one of his own. He had to see those breasts.

Jerking up her shirt with his free hand, he saw the low cut of her bra, which barely covered her nipples. Thankfully, it had a front clasp. He popped the clasp and pushed the lacy material away.

"Beautiful," he murmured, taking a second to glance at her face. Her lids were heavy with passion, and he felt a rush of wicked pleasure as his tongue darted out to flick her stiffened peaks.

Shelly's back arched, thrusting her breasts farther into his face. He caught her light, flowery scent, and his urge to bury himself inside her intensified.

When he returned his lips to her mouth, they surged against each other. Their mouths sucked and licked and nipped until he felt his knees begin to weaken.

With all his energy centered at his groin, he was forced to let her slide down the wall to her feet. But her legs wouldn't support her, and she continued down until she was sitting on the floor.

Linc followed her down, laying her out on the hard wood of his foyer. Then he covered her with his body. Licking her neck just under her jaw, he slipped his hand between them and began to fiddle with the zipper of her jeans.

As his weight pressed her to the floor, she groaned. But his mind—hazed with desire—didn't register it as pain until she asked, "Any chance we can continue this somewhere more comfortable?"

Realizing that she was squirming and arching her back in discomfort, he quickly lifted her up and swung her into his arms. "Yes, of course. Let's go to my bedroom."

Shelly held her shirt closed with one hand and wrapped the other around Linc's neck as he carried her to his bedroom. Her mind was a whirlwind.

This was really going to happen. Anticipation had ruled her thoughts all day, but she hadn't expected for things to move so fast. There wasn't any time to think.

Linc placed her into a sitting position on his king-size bed and then pulled off her shirt and her bra. Her first instinct was to feel self-conscious, but the look of worship in his eyes as he took in her bare torso relaxed her.

Next, he went to work on her jeans. She kicked off her tennis shoes and raised her hips to help him peel them from her body.

When his hands started reaching for her panties, she evaded his grasp. Instead, she came to her feet and slipped her fingers under his skintight T-shirt, which molded every muscle in his chest. He helped her pull it over his head, and then it was her turn to work on his jeans.

He stepped free of the denim, revealing hip-hugging boxer briefs and sculpted thighs and calves. Feeling wicked, Shelly looked him in the eyes as she hooked her fingers in his briefs and pulled them down his legs.

He returned her gaze boldly as he tugged at the fabric

of her panties, and the lacy strings holding them together gave way. The torn scrap of fabric fell to her feet, but there wasn't time to feel outrage at the loss of her favorite panties.

Linc hoisted her onto the bed, flat on her back, then came down on top of her. Their mouths and tongues came together again and again as he cupped her breasts and she reached for any smooth skin she could find.

Finally, when Shelly was writhing and whispering his name with a sense of urgency, Linc retrieved a condom from his bedside table. He put it on quickly and spread her legs for his entry. As Shelly felt him filling her, a surge of pleasure shot through her.

They were both anxious, thrusting their bodies together as if the contact would never be enough. Finally, Shelly felt her climax beginning to build. As if sensing her need, Linc increased their friction, doubling the pressure mounting inside her.

He held her tightly as she cried out, her pleasure complete. As her body continued to spasm, she watched Linc's face contort in his own ecstasy as he released a long moan of satisfaction.

Shelly woke up before Linc, with her stomach rumbling for food. She almost never wanted breakfast in the morning, but she also almost never had such a vigorous workout long into the night.

After they'd made love the first time, Shelly and Linc had retrieved their dinners from the oven and dined on the bed, picnic style. When their stomachs were full, they were tired. They'd made slow, leisurely love before falling asleep for the night.

Climbing out of bed, Shelly made a beeline to the

bathroom. Her hair was mussed, and her braids were beginning to unravel. Quickly unbraiding her pigtails, she finger combed her hair until it looked more presentable. Then she belted her short silk robe around her waist to protect herself from the chill of the air conditioner.

Shelly wasn't sure what she would find in Linc's refrigerator, but she was hungry enough to go foraging for leftovers.

Walking into the kitchen, she was startled to see someone standing in front of the stove. The person's identity didn't register in her sleep-addled brain, and she let loose an earsplitting shriek.

The woman jumped into the air, screaming herself and throwing an empty baking pan toward the ceiling. Both women clutched their chests, taking each other in with wide eyes.

Shelly instantly realized that the plump, olive-skinned woman had to be Linc's housekeeper. "Oh, my gosh. You must be Adelina. I'm so sorry I scared you. I'm Shelly."

Shelly had prepared herself for a number of responses, from anger to indifference. But she wasn't prepared for Adelina to cup her cheeks and pull Shelly's head into her ample bosom.

"Shelly, oh, how wonderful to have you here."

Shelly lifted her head. "Thank you, Adelina. Once again, I'm so sorry I startled you. I just wasn't expecting to find anyone in here so early. Um, what's wrong?"

Adelina was still cupping Shelly's cheeks and gazing up at her with unshed tears in her eyes. "Nothing is wrong. I'm just so happy for my Lincoln. He has finally found love."

Shelly felt her face heat up. "What makes you say that?"

"Because you are here. He has never let a woman stay long enough for me to see her. I know that means you are very special."

Tamping down the unexpected pleasure Adelina's words had given her, Shelly tried to keep things in perspective. "I don't know about that. We haven't been…a couple for very long."

"Trust me. I know these things," Adelina said, turning toward the refrigerator. "Now, I brought groceries this morning. I can make anything you want for breakfast. Pancakes, eggs, French toast… What would you like?"

"Oh, no, Adelina. I don't expect you to cook for me. I'll be fine with a cup of coffee and some toast."

"Nonsense. You need a good breakfast. What do you like?"

Realizing the older woman was determined to feed her, Shelly finally said, "Please, don't go to any trouble. I'll have whatever you would have made for Linc."

"His favorite is huevos rancheros. Fried tortillas and eggs with a tomato-chili sauce. I serve it with refried beans and potatoes."

Shelly's stomach rumbled again. "Mmm. That sounds wonderful, Adelina. Thank you."

While Adelina bustled about the kitchen, preparing breakfast, Shelly pulled herself up onto a stool to watch. Their conversation fell into an easy rhythm, and before long, Adelina was regaling her with stories of Linc's teen years on the ranch.

"He fell off the horse and into a pile of cow manure," Adelina said at the end of one of her stories.

Shelly was wiping tears of laughter from her eyes as Linc entered the kitchen. He paused in the doorway, shaking his head.

"This is exactly why I never let my girlfriends get anywhere near you, Adelina," he commented.

He walked over to Shelly and kissed her on the cheek and then crossed to the stove to do the same to Adelina.

Shelly's heart was hammering. So it was true. Was she really his girlfriend?

"Ahh, I see you're making huevos rancheros. What did I do to deserve this?" Linc asked.

Shelly frowned. "What do you mean? She said it was your favorite."

Linc rubbed his stomach. "That's right, but she hardly ever makes it for me. It's not my birthday. It's not Christmas—"

"I'm celebrating Shelly's visit. You be good to her, Lincoln. I like her," Adelina replied.

Shelly beamed at him, and he shook his head. "You're already turning her against me. I guess I know when I'm outnumbered."

The three of them sat down at the dining table for breakfast and enjoyed Adelina's delicious meal. Despite his best protests, his housekeeper continued to spill all of Linc's childhood secrets. Shelly relished the comfortable family atmosphere, an atmosphere that she hadn't felt in years, if ever.

Suddenly missing her own family, she made a mental note to call her mother as soon as she got back home.

"Where are we going?" Shelly asked Linc later that afternoon. He'd saddled up a horse for her, and now she was riding behind him along a private trail.

"It's a surprise."

While she'd been getting dressed, he'd jumped into his pickup truck and set up a romantic lunch by the creek.

A few minutes later they broke through the trees and trotted into a clearing that faced the water. "Here we are," Linc announced.

"Oh, my goodness! When did you find the time to do this?"

"I had to move quickly while you were showering."

He'd spread a picnic cloth on several bales of hay, leaving two bales for them to sit on. Inside a cooler, he'd packed some of Adelina's best summer dishes, like potato salad, roasted chicken and corn muffins. He had a sweet wine and fruit for dessert.

They tethered their horses and sat down to eat. Shelly smiled at him as he placed a filled plate in front of her. "I never would have guessed you were such a romantic."

He paused to think about that. He knew how to buy fancy dinners at expensive restaurants, and occasionally, he'd splurge on gifts, because he thought it was expected, but he'd never gone to this much trouble on a date before.

Shelly was definitely bringing out the best in him. For years, he'd lived in fear of Adelina spilling the embarrassing secrets of his youth to a date, as she had today. But now that it had happened, he didn't mind, after all. The truth was, he'd loved it. Seeing the two of them together had just felt right.

"It was just a simple statement. I didn't expect it to send you into a mental coma," said Shelly, interrupting his thoughts.

"No, I was just thinking that I never considered myself much of a romantic before today, either. But I got the idea on the phone yesterday. It seems you have a thing for fields and haystacks." He watched Shelly blush. "What is it?"

"Maybe after I've had a little more wine, I'll tell you. Not yet. Right now, I want to hear all about you."

"Didn't you get enough dirt out of Adelina this morning?"

"She told me some things, but I still have questions. You don't have to tell me if you don't want to, but what happened to your parents?"

Linc took a deep breath. He was hoping to be numb when it came to discussing his parents' fates now that so many years had passed, but thinking about them still made his chest burn.

"My parents were divorced when I was three, and I moved to Detroit to live with my mother. We didn't have a lot of money, so we didn't live in the best neighborhood. When I was thirteen, my mother was killed in a grocery-store robbery. She was there only because I'd begged her to bring me my favorite cereal, Honey Crunchios. To this day, I can't stand the sight of Honey Crunchios."

"Oh my God. I'm so sorry. But you can't blame yourself. She was in the wrong place at the wrong time."

Linc didn't allow himself to look at her. "It's okay. I worked all that out in the intervening years. After my mother died, I came here to live on this ranch with my dad. I hated it at first. I'd started getting involved with the wrong crowd in Detroit, and I thought I was a badass.

"But my father wasn't having it. I had daily chores, hard, backbreaking work, and I had to study every night until I brought all my grades up to *A*s. Before then I had never thought I was smart, and I didn't know I was capable of getting those kinds of grades. He changed my life. He taught me that I could do anything if I worked hard enough. Unfortunately, he never got to see what he'd molded me into. He died of a heart attack during my senior year in college."

"Trust me," Shelly said. "I'm sure he knows."

"Well, that's my life story in a nutshell. What about you? Are you close to your parents?" Linc asked, glad to be off the hot seat.

She furrowed her brow. "My parents got divorced when I was young. Afterward, my dad just disappeared. Right now I couldn't tell you where he is if my life depended on it. For years, I blamed my mother. She worked so much, she never had time for the family. She and I had a very rocky relationship. But now that I'm an adult, we've worked through our problems, and we get along much better. Sylvia is more like my friend than a mother now."

Linc smiled. "You call your mother by her first name?"

"After she got remarried, she tried to get us to do it. But I still can't say it to her face," she said, becoming quiet for a minute. Then she looked up suddenly. "Hey, I have another question."

Linc held his breath, hoping it didn't have anything to do with his parents. "Go ahead."

"What is that giant covered wagon in your stable used for? I got the impression that aside from the horses, this isn't much of a working ranch anymore."

Linc felt heat rising up his neck. "It's for camp."

"Camp? What do you mean?"

The cat was out of the bag now. "Every summer we bus in kids from the inner cities to attend a week of camp here. It gives them a chance to experience the outdoors, with plenty of room to run around. They play with the animals and learn about ranch life. It's run by the professional camp organization Wide Open Spaces. They bring most of what they need. I just let them use my property."

Shelly was looking at him with doe eyes. "That sounds wonderful. Though something tells me you're being modest."

"Who me? The cocky, arrogant astronaut? Never."

They finished their lunch, and Linc knew it was his turn to put Shelly back on the spot. "Now I want to hear all about this fascination you have with hay bales."

Getting up, she came to settle herself on his lap. Then she proceeded to tell him all about the naughty dream she'd had recently.

A wicked smile curved his lips. "And just what do you plan to do about that now that you're here?"

She began unbuttoning his shirt. "Ride 'em, cowboy!"

Shelly was still picking straw from her hair when they returned to the house just before sunset. After spending a long day outdoors, romping in the heat, she was exhausted.

"I think I'm going to take a shower, in case I've got some stray hay lurking somewhere," she announced.

Linc followed her into the bedroom. "I think I'll join you."

She shot him a suspicious look. "Okay, but this shower is just for getting clean. Nothing else."

He laughed. "What? Don't you trust me?"

Before she could answer him, his phone started ringing. She noticed her cell phone was ringing as well.

Linc crossed the room to answer his line, while she flipped the cover on her cell. "Hello?"

"Shelly, we're going to need you to come into work tomorrow morning. There's been an accident." It was one of the project leaders on GRM.

"What kind of accident?"

"Dusty Chambers was in a car accident."

Shelly hung up the phone and turned to Linc, who'd just ended his call, and they exchanged looks of concern. "I have to go to work tomorrow."

He nodded. "So do I."

Chapter 9

He was back on the mission. Stepping outside the conference room, Linc took a minute to let that knowledge sink in.

He'd shown up at Johnson Space Center that morning, uncertain of what to expect. Right away, he'd been ushered into a closed meeting and informed that the Alpha and the Beta teams would be combined. Linc would pilot Draco, and Vince and Paul of the Beta team would continue in their roles as copilot and mission specialist.

Fortunately, Dustin Chambers would fully recover from his accident, but with a broken arm and three cracked ribs, he wouldn't be returning to the mission.

This wasn't the way Linc had wanted to get back into space, but he had a job to do. If someone really was trying to sabotage this mission, they were going to have a much more difficult time of it from now on. New security badges were being passed out, and only essential personnel would be cleared for each area.

Shelly filed out of the conference room with some of the others, and Linc tugged on her elbow to stop her. "Can you believe—"

She swiped his hand away. "Not now. I'll talk to you later," she muttered under her breath.

Linc watched her walk away, shaking his head. He should have expected this. She'd only agreed to date him once he'd been pulled from GRM. Now that they would be working together again, it was clear that she was pulling away.

Linc forced himself not to dwell on it as he rushed through the day, taking security photos, filling out paperwork and signing confidentiality agreements. Tomorrow they would run the launch separation test again.

Back home that evening, Linc found himself struggling with a problem he'd never had before. Fear. After the last accident, he was starting to worry about all the possible outcomes of the launch separation test.

In the past, he'd never given a second thought to his safety or what could go wrong on a mission. Now, suddenly, he had someone in his life that he cared about. Someone he wanted to come home to.

Linc shook his head, berating himself for getting emotional. Here he was, falling in love with Shelly, and she could barely tolerate being seen with him at work. How had he allowed this to happen? It was probably just a matter of time before she formally broke things off.

He was jerked out of his reverie when the doorbell rang. When he pulled the door open and saw it was Shelly, he was certain his fears were about to become a reality.

"Hey." His voice came out heavier than he'd expected. "I was just thinking about you."

A smile broke across her lips. "Good, because I was thinking about you." She held out two bags of carryout. "I brought you dinner from Moe's. I thought we could eat together."

Instantly, Linc's heart felt lighter. Shelly wasn't pulling away, after all. Maybe she just wanted to maintain their space at work.

He set down her bags and pulled her into his arms. "We can eat in a minute. First, I just want to hold you."

She went into his arms willingly, and Linc savored the moment. He held her as long as was comfortable; then they moved into the living room and unpacked the carryout on his coffee table.

"I guess your theory about Dusty sabotaging the project is blown now," Shelly said between bites of her barbecue sandwich. "I never was too convinced that he was our man. Sure, the two of you didn't always get along, but I would never question his loyalty to NASA."

Linc shook his head. "I can't explain the weird vibe I've always gotten from him, though. He gave me the impression that he'd be more than happy to see me taken down a notch. So much so that he might have been willing to do the job himself."

Shelly frowned at him. "You guys are always telling me that a little competition is common in the military, and especially among astronauts."

He stared at his food. "I don't know. If you think about it, just because he had a car accident doesn't mean he didn't try to sabotage the mission. Maybe he just got the brunt of his own bad karma. The car accident foiled his plot."

She sighed. "I think you should leave the sleuthing to the professionals. With all the new security measures in place, there won't be any more incidents like the last one. The person responsible was probably some low-level tech that was paid off. Someone like that won't get anywhere near Draco now."

"I hope you're right. We can't afford to lose any more time."

Linc didn't want to think about possible problems with the mission anymore. He wanted answers, which only Shelly could give him.

"Can I ask you a question?"

Shelly dabbed her mouth with a napkin. "What's up?"

"Were you avoiding me at work today?"

He saw her avert her gaze in embarrassment. "I wasn't trying to avoid you. But I do think it's important that we keep our relationship on the down low. You already know how I feel about this. I expected you to understand."

"It's not that I don't understand. I know you're worried about being taken seriously as a professional. And, I'm certainly not trying to interfere with that. But I don't think that means you have to pretend you don't know me."

She shrugged. "I don't think I did that, but if that's how it seemed, I'm sorry. Doesn't showing up with dinner make up for any unintentional offense I may have committed?"

Linc wiped off his hands and pushed himself back from the coffee table. "No. If you want to make up for your offenses, it's going to take a lot more than dinner."

Laughing, Shelly raised her face to his kiss. "Don't worry. I always pay my debts."

* * *

Shelly held her breath throughout the second launch separation test. It had been harrowing to watch the vehicle Linc was in catch fire the first time, and that was all she could think about during the second simulation.

Thankfully, everything worked as planned, and the mission was back on track. The new security measures were working, and even though it troubled her not to know the identity of the saboteur, it felt good to know the project wouldn't be canceled.

But balancing work and her relationship with Linc was a struggle. It had taken all her inner will not to show her emotions on her face when Linc emerged from the simulator, unscathed, during the second launch simulation test. All she'd wanted to do was run to him and throw her arms around him.

Instead, she'd hurried to the ladies' room to collect herself. Shelly knew Linc didn't like the fact that she was keeping her distance at work, but it was the only way she knew to cope with the situation. They could both be reprimanded if their relationship was discovered.

Fortunately, she was sent to the Mojave Desert for two days to supervise Draco's final inspection. That gave her a break from Linc and her juggling act. The only downside was that she would miss two days of training in the Neutral Buoyancy Lab.

A replica of Draco and Guardian, the satellite that needed repair, had been submerged in the NBL's large pool. The underwater environment simulated the weightlessness in space, allowing the astronauts to practice their extravehicular activities as realistically as possible.

She hated missing the first two days of NBL training. Since all the phases of Draco's construction had gone perfectly, Shelly decided to leave the Mojave Desert early. She wanted to get back to Houston in time to observe the rest of the NBL training exercises.

Driving to the building that housed the NBL's pool, Shelly could barely contain her excitement. She'd spent a lot of time adjusting the maneuverability of Draco's extension arm, but she didn't have any idea how it would be used to repair the satellite.

She crossed the lobby at a brisk pace, hoping she hadn't missed too much already. She swiped her security badge and pulled the door handle. The light on the panel blinked red.

Frowning, Shelly swiped her badge again. She must have rushed the first time. Once again, the light blinked red, and the door remained closed.

"There must be some mistake," she muttered to herself. Taking out her cell phone, she dialed the administration office.

"GRM. This is Melissa speaking."

"Hi, Melissa. This is Shelly. I'm trying to get into the Neutral Buoyancy Lab, but my badge isn't working. Can you check on my clearance?"

"No problem." Melissa put her on hold for a moment. "Shelly, my records show that you were never granted NBL access."

"You mean since the new security protocols were made, right?"

"Actually, from the start of the project. The NBL has a top-level security clearance. Military personnel only."

Feeling her spine go numb, Shelly muttered, "Okay. Thanks, Melissa."

Shelly went back to her desk and spent the afternoon on the phone, trying to get answers from Colonel Murphy or one of the other directors. Everyone she tried to reach was in the lab and inaccessible. All she could do was leave messages for someone to call her back.

Back at home that evening, Shelly still couldn't get this off her mind. Why would she be denied access to a major portion of Draco's training? When she was given the job, no one had said anything about restricting her access. In fact, she'd spent a significant amount of time working on design revisions specifically for the underwater testing.

Knowing she wouldn't get a good night's sleep, she picked up the phone and dialed Linc's number.

"Shelly, you're home. I thought you weren't due back from California until next week."

"Is that what they told you?"

"Uh…yeah."

"I came back early because I didn't want to miss all the NBL training."

Linc was silent on the other end.

"Did you know that I wasn't given clearance to observe the exercises?" she asked.

"Um, I thought that was why you were in the desert."

"So you did know."

"I don't know what you want me to tell you, Shelly. None of this is up to me. And, I really can't give you the answers you want. Colonel Murphy is the only person who can do that."

"Can you at least tell me why only military personnel have been cleared?"

"Shelly, you know I can't. Talk to Colonel Murphy," he advised.

Shelly hung up the phone. "You better believe I will."

* * *

It took her two days, but Shelly finally arranged a meeting to discuss her concerns with Colonel Murphy. As she entered his office, she was surprised to see that Linc was already there.

She took her place beside him, with an uneasy feeling growing in her chest. Before she could open her mouth, Colonel Murphy was speaking.

"Commander Ripley has explained that you have some concerns about your security clearance."

Shelly nodded. "That's right."

"Shelly, these security measures were in place from the start. You shouldn't take it personally that you don't have access," Colonel Murphy stated.

"Can you at least tell me *why* I don't have access?" Shelly asked.

"Those answers come with clearance," said the colonel.

Linc leaned forward. "Colonel, is there any way Shelly's clearance could be upgraded? She does have a pivotal role in this training process, and you already know that we've had a few problems with the extension arm over the last few days. If Shelly had been permitted to be present, we may have resolved these issues faster."

The colonel rubbed his forehead. "That decision really isn't up to me."

"With all due respect, sir, I'm certain that if you requested that Shelly's clearance be upgraded, your superiors would respect your authority," said Linc.

Shelly bit her lip, resisting the urge to hug Linc. She'd never expected him to stick up for her like this.

With a heavy sigh, Colonel Murphy said, "Let me make a few phone calls. I'll get back to you."

Later that afternoon, Shelly was called back into the colonel's office. Once again, Linc was there.

Shelly took a seat, but Colonel Murphy remained standing, pacing the room. "Commander Ripley helped me make the case for upgrading your security clearance to the executive committee."

She slid to the edge of her seat. "And?"

"And, by tomorrow morning you'll have access to the NBL so you can help troubleshoot any further glitches with Draco's extension arm," announced the colonel.

Shelly brought her hands together with excitement. "That's great. Thank you so much, Colonel Murphy, and thank you, Linc."

She gave Linc a sidelong glance and noted that he still wasn't smiling. "There's more, Shelly."

"There's a reason the Neutral Buoyancy Lab has been restricted. It's the same reason Draco can be manned only by military personnel," said the colonel.

Shelly got a sinking feeling in the pit of her stomach. "I'm listening."

"Guardian is a satellite that was placed into space by the National Reconnaissance Office," explained the colonel.

She nodded. "Yes, it's a spy satellite."

"It's more than just a spy satellite, Shelly," Linc said.

"That's right," Colonel Murphy added. "It's imperative that Guardian doesn't crash to earth. It's not only dangerous, but there are serious security issues."

A startling thought came to her, crawling up her spine like a nasty creature. Draco's mission specialist was a weapons expert.

"There's something on Guardian that you don't want people to see, isn't there?" she asked.

Colonel Murphy stopped pacing. "Guardian was deployed in the mideighties as part of SDI, the Strategic Defense Initiative. There are serious military applications on board."

Shelly lost her breath. She could read between the lines. "Are you talking about nuclear ballistic missiles? Star Wars is real? Everyone was led to believe that program was never fully developed."

Both men in the room were silent.

Shelly wiped her hands over her face, unable to believe what she was hearing. "Are there others? Are there other satellites in space armed with missiles?"

The colonel moved behind his desk, no longer meeting her eyes. "To the best of my knowledge, Guardian was a prototype for SDI. In any case, our mission directive is clear. Guardian cannot be allowed to crash to earth."

Shelly just sat there, shaking her head. No one in the room had confirmed that there were missiles on board Guardian, but no one had denied it.

"So, obviously, the reason I needed higher clearance was that the NBL training focuses on disarming the missiles." Her head snapped up as she worked through it in her mind. "Why don't you just shoot Guardian down?"

"The United States government's official position is that Guardian doesn't exist. Shooting it down would raise too many questions," explained the colonel.

"Okay," Shelly finally said, when her brain reached overload. "Thank you for telling me."

Colonel Murphy exchanged a look with Linc. "Be careful what you wish for. Now you've got to carry this burden like the rest of us."

* * *

Linc stood on Shelly's doorstep, debating whether or not to ring the bell. He'd nearly changed his mind a hundred times on the drive over, but he'd finally decided that she had a right to know the truth.

But now that it was time to face her, he wasn't sure that he was doing the right thing. She'd already had an emotionally overwhelming day. What he had to say to her would only make it worse.

He came to the sudden realization that just because he'd gotten his answers today didn't mean it was the right time to give them to Shelly. There was no immediate need for her to know. In fact, maybe the best time to fill her in was after the mission was over.

Kicking himself for taking so long to come to a definitive decision, Linc started back to his car just as Shelly's front door opened.

She poked her head out. "What are you doing? Are you leaving?"

"Uh…how did you know I was here?"

"I heard your car pull up. I've been standing in the foyer for the last two minutes, waiting for you to ring the bell. Aren't you going to come in?"

Realizing the choice had been taken out of his hands, he followed her into the house. "I had just convinced myself that coming over here was a mistake."

"Why? Did you think I wouldn't want to see you because you were obligated by your job to withhold a juicy government secret from me?"

He sat down with her on the sofa. "No. Because you're probably on emotional overload, and I should give you some time to process what you've learned."

Shelly blew out her breath. "It was shocking. I mean, we all question how much our government is telling us, but you never really want to believe they have secrets of this magnitude."

Linc nodded. "Once the blinders are off, you can't put them back on again. Do you wish you'd never learned the truth?"

She vehemently shook her head. "No, I'm not the kind of person who likes to bury her head in the sand. Even though it's a lot to take in, it means a lot to me that you helped convince Colonel Murphy to confide in me. Knowing the truth is better than walking around in a fog of ignorant bliss."

Linc studied her face. She seemed to really mean it. But that didn't mean her philosophy would apply to her personal life. "Do you feel that way about everything? Would you still want to know the truth even if it changed the way you felt about someone close to you?"

She didn't hesitate. "Especially then."

That was the opening he needed. He'd just have to tell her the truth and hope she stood by her words. "Well, in that case, I have something else to tell you."

She sat up straight. "Are you afraid what you're going to tell me will change the way I feel about you? Is that why I caught you sneaking back to your car?"

Linc rubbed the stubble on his chin, trying to stall. "Not exactly. What I have to tell you isn't about me. It's about something very important to you."

"I can't take any more suspense. Just say it."

"When you told me about your applications to the astronaut program, I thought it was suspicious that someone with your qualifications hadn't made it further in the process. So, I made a few calls—"

"And?" Shelly asked, pressing him, clearly running low on patience.

"I know why you've been rejected from the astronaut program three times. And why you'll continue to be rejected in the future."

Shelly's face fell. "What is it?" she asked, her voice breathy.

"You've been blackballed. Apparently, someone in Congress has been using their authority to keep you out of the program," Linc hedged, not wanting to give the name outright.

He'd expected some form of denial or even lashing out, but he was not prepared for the cold chill that surrounded her next words.

"And let me guess who that person is. My mother."

Chapter 10

Shelly launched herself from the sofa, her rising anger overtaking any feelings of shock or betrayal. "I should have known," she said, pacing in front of Linc. "When the space shuttle *Columbia* blew up, my mother went into a tailspin. She tried everything she could to convince me to pursue another career. I knew she was worried about me going into space and never coming back, but I had no idea that she'd go to these lengths to keep me grounded."

Linc lowered his head in obvious regret. "I'm sorry I had to be the one to tell you."

She came to a stop in front of him. "Oh, no, don't apologize. You've just done me the biggest favor of my life. Now that I know what's been standing in my way—or should I say *who*—I can make her fix it."

"Are you going to call her?"

"And give her the chance to dodge me? No, I've got to confront her in person." She resumed pacing back and forth across the room, an outlet for her pent-up fury. "I've got to do it as soon as possible, too. I need to go to Washington."

Linc stood. "I could fly you."

She stopped. "You wouldn't mind?"

"Of course not. We can leave tomorrow night, after work, and be back before training resumes Monday morning."

Watching Linc's face, which was lined with concern, Shelly moved toward him. "Thank you for checking into this and for telling me the truth. Now I can understand why you would hesitate to lay this on me. And I appreciate you trusting me to be able to handle it."

He pulled her into his arms. "Shelly, I'll always have your back. Remember that."

Her muscles were tight and tense, but in Linc's arms, she began to relax. Without thinking, she raised her face to his for a kiss.

Their lips came together in soft pecks, which gradually grew longer and more urgent. Feeling that familiar stir of excitement in her belly, Shelly grabbed at Linc's shirt. She didn't want to waste time running to the bedroom. She wanted her release right then and there.

Her fingers were clumsy, and her hands fumbled in their haste to peel off his clothes, so Linc took over when it was her turn to disrobe. He carefully undressed her down to the skin, then leaned back on the sofa, settling her on his lap.

Shelly wanted to get lost in him. Soft skin. Hard muscles. Sharp, masculine angles. His kisses were drugging, and she didn't have to think. His body did all the work. Moving her into position. Stroking her into a feverish state.

Their bodies joined, and as Linc guided her hips faster and faster over his, Shelly let herself go.

No matter what tomorrow brought, today her world was Lincoln Ripley.

Despite Linc's best efforts to cheer her up during the flight to Washington, D.C., Shelly was in no mood for small talk. Not wanting to hurt his feelings, she finally had to pretend to sleep to be alone with her thoughts.

Shelly's entire world had changed in twenty-four hours. She couldn't even recognize the truth anymore. It was hard not to question all of her relationships.

Finding out that her government had armed missiles circling the earth was shattering enough. Finding out that her mother had denied her the one thing she'd been working for her entire life was too much.

She didn't even know what she would say to her mother. Part of her never wanted to speak to that woman again, but an even bigger part of her needed answers. Those answers were bound to leave her empty, but she needed them all the same.

Once they landed at Andrews Air Force Base, Linc took a cab to a hotel, and Shelly took one to her mother's home in Chevy Chase, Maryland.

Taking a deep breath, she rang the doorbell, and it was answered moments later by her stepfather, Charles.

"Shelly, what a surprise. Sylvia will be thrilled to see you. To what do we owe this unexpected pleasure?"

"Hi, Charles," Shelly said, walking past him and into the foyer. They were friendly with each other, but they'd never progressed to the hugging stage. "I have something to talk to my mother about, and it couldn't wait."

A wary look crossed his eyes. "Okay. Why don't you make yourself comfortable in the living room, and I'll let her know you're here."

Shelly crossed the white carpet to the white sofa and sat down. Everything in this room was formal and uptight, just like her mother.

Minutes later her perfectly groomed silver-haired mother entered the room. "Sweetheart, what a surprise," she said, moving toward Shelly, arms wide for a hug.

Shelly entered her embrace out of habit and obligation. She wasn't feeling particularly warm toward her mother at that moment.

"Why didn't you tell me you were coming for a visit?" asked Sylvia.

"Because it's not so much a visit as a confrontation, *Mother*." She emphasized the last word, knowing it would tip her mother off to her mood.

"Honey, you sound upset. What's wrong?"

Shelly hadn't practiced a speech, and all the words that had been circling in her brain during the flight were nowhere to be found now that she needed them.

Sylvia was staring her down with that cool, dark gaze she used to push bills through Congress. It was more than a little intimidating.

"I got some interesting news," Shelly began, trying to build up her nerve.

Sylvia clutched her chest. "Oh my God. Are you pregnant?"

Shelly rolled her eyes. "No, actually, this is about my career. I found out why I haven't been able to get into the astronaut program."

To her mother's credit, her face gave nothing away. She just waited.

Her lack of reaction pushed Shelly's temper to the edge. "It seems you've been using your influence to keep me out. And, for the life of me, I can't figure out why you'd do such a horrible thing."

Sylvia sat down on the sofa. "Shelly, I knew if you ever found out, you'd have trouble understanding my position, but I really was just trying to do what's best for you."

Shelly's entire body went hot. At least Sylvia hadn't denied it. She'd half expected Sylvia to try and convince her that she'd gotten her facts wrong.

But the truth was of little comfort. "How is ruining my lifelong dream what's best for me?"

"Astronauts have a dangerous job. There's a very real chance that you could go into space and never come back."

"And there's a very real chance I could get hit by a bus. I'm thirty years old. I'm way past needing you to shield me from all the dangers in life." Shelly felt herself shaking.

"Shelly, after *Columbia* blew up, I knew I could never live with the same thing happening to you. Charles and I had just gotten married, and our family was just beginning to come together. I didn't want anything to destroy that."

"You didn't even give me the chance to find out if I could have made it on my own. Maybe your wish would have come true, and they would have denied me, anyway. You didn't allow me to try," she said in a low voice, trying to control her temper.

"You've had a very successful career as an aerospace engineer. If you think about it, you might decide that it's enough for you. You could settle down long enough to get married and have a family. Being an astronaut is too risky for a mother, and I'd like grandchildren."

Shelly jumped up to stare down at her mother. "Am I seriously hearing this right now? You're supposed to be a modern woman—an advocate for women's rights— but you're actually telling me to content myself with having a family because my career is too dangerous."

"That's not what I'm saying. I just think you're too focused. Your life needs a little balance. I don't want you to make the mistakes I made. There are so many things I'd do differently if I had the chance. Spending more time with my children is number one."

Exasperated, Shelly sat back down. "What gives you the right to decide what my future will be? It would have been fine if I'd been rejected because I just wasn't good enough. But to find out that I was being held back by my mother—a woman who sacrificed a lot for her own career. Do you know what a betrayal that is?"

Sylvia just shook her head. "When you have children, you'll understand. And I'm so worried that you won't allow yourself that chance."

"That's ridiculous. I'd never do such a thing to someone I loved, especially my children—if I choose to have any. Have you been in politics for so long that you actually think what you did is okay? Deciding what's right and wrong regardless of what a person really wants?"

"I'm sorry—"

"Wow. I wasn't expecting that." She couldn't keep the sarcasm out of her voice. "But you really *should* be sorry, Mother. Do you know how much I've doubted myself? How hopeless I was beginning to feel because no matter how hard I worked, I couldn't get close to my dream?"

Her mother covered her knee with her hand. "I never meant to make you feel insecure. I know it was selfish of me. I can't give you a better explanation."

"I'm past explanations, anyway," Shelly said. "I want your word that you're going to undo the damage you've done. Pull all the strings, and call in all the favors it takes to get me a fair shot. If you can't make this right, I'll never be able to forgive you."

"Shelly, please don't be hasty—"

"I don't want to hear anything but your word, Mother. I need you to fix this."

After a long silence, Sylvia finally nodded. "I promise."

When Shelly arrived at the hotel, she was both physically and emotionally exhausted.

Linc had been sprawled across the bed, watching television. He sat up as she entered the room. "How did it go?"

Shelly shook her head. She couldn't find the words to talk about it. Part of her wished that she'd come alone to Washington, just so she wouldn't have any witnesses to her volatile emotions. Linc meant well, but how could she talk about something she couldn't even understand herself?

"Did your mother admit what she did?" he asked.

Shelly nodded, crawling on the bed and turning her back to him. She felt his fingers kneading her shoulders, and her back stiffened. "I'm really tired. Do you mind if I take a nap?"

"Sure. No problem. I'll let you rest," he said, moving off the bed.

As Linc watched Shelly's sleeping form, he realized that nothing about this trip was going the way he'd expected. She'd barely spoken to him on the flight to D.C., and now that she'd made it to the hotel, she still didn't want to talk.

Not wanting to prowl around the room alone, Linc got into the elevator and headed down to the lobby. He'd known it would be an emotional time. But he'd looked forward to being Shelly's support system. He'd expected her to return from an emotional confrontation with her mother and cry on his shoulder. Instead, he felt her pulling away.

She had stiffened when he touched her, and she wouldn't confide in him. He was new to serious relationships, but he'd always believed it was the tough times that were supposed to bring couples together. That is, if their love was strong enough.

Linc found himself heading out the front door of the hotel and into the night. He didn't know his way around the streets of D.C., but if he circled the block, he probably wouldn't get into too much trouble. The late spring air was warm, and the sidewalks were alive with people heading off to one party scene or another.

As much as he tried to focus on his surroundings, the buildings, the cars, the people, one thought kept intruding itself into his mind.

Did Shelly love him?

He hadn't even had the nerve to tell her that he was in love with her. Part of him thought that she wouldn't believe him, or that she'd take it as a joke, if he did. He'd never let himself wade in this deep. He didn't want to bare all until he knew Shelly was ready to accept him.

Maybe she thought he was still the hotshot player she believed him to be from the start. It was possible that all she really wanted was a good time.

Linc was so lost in his thoughts, he almost got clipped by a cab as he shuffled across the street. Snapping to attention, he realized he wasn't in the right frame of mind to wander aimlessly.

He passed several restaurants with outdoor seating and finally stumbled upon a bar with funky music spilling out onto the street.

On impulse, he walked in and miraculously found an empty seat at the bar. He held up a twenty-dollar bill and waited. It took several minutes, but a harried bartender finally caught his eye, and Linc ordered an imported beer.

Glancing around the room at the fabric-draped walls and the trendy decor of colorful velvet sofas and crazy S-shaped plastic chairs, Linc missed his favorite local bar, Boondoggles.

It was simple and unpretentious, and he could have been there right now, knocking back a brew in his custom stein with his buddies. In his pre-Shelly life, there was no rejection, none of this confusion and no chance of getting his heart broken.

Linc hadn't been at the bar ten minutes before a sexy blonde approached him. She looked like Scarlett Johansson and was dressed in a low-cut blouse and tight jeans.

"You look really familiar. Are you a celebrity?" she asked, batting her mascara-coated lashes at him.

Linc took in those flirty eyes and pouty lips, and warning bells went off. Something about this situation was so familiar, and yet it felt so wrong.

"Damn, you guessed my secret," he said as the bartender set his beer in front of him. "Now that I've been discovered, I have to leave. Enjoy this beer on me. I've got to get out of here before the paparazzi find me."

Linc made his hasty exit, leaving the blonde's head spinning with confusion.

The fact was, he wasn't about to give up on Shelly.

He knew she was under a lot of stress. It had been a difficult week, and he'd compounded that by telling her the truth about her mother. Maybe she was starting to resent the fact that he'd piled more on her already full plate.

There was still a chance that her sour mood would sweeten after some rest. When Linc returned to the hotel room, he saw that Shelly had awakened from her nap just long enough to have a room-service dinner. And now she was back in bed, sound asleep.

Linc undressed and climbed into bed beside her. Tomorrow Shelly was supposed to take him to meet her sister. He couldn't help hoping that a glimpse into Shelly's family life would help him figure her out.

Shelly woke up the next morning and went through her morning routine like a robot. Her mind was so weighed down, and her heart was so heavy, she felt like a rain cloud was hanging over her.

As much as she wanted to see Cheryl today, she couldn't help wishing she'd never made these plans. If she was going to get through the day, she was going to have to pretend everything was fine. And Shelly knew her sister would see right through her mask.

Linc tried to make small talk on the cab ride to her sister's house, near Dupont Circle, but Shelly wanted for all the world to be left alone. Instead, she tried her best to answer his questions, although her responses sounded curt to her own ears.

She knew she was shutting him out, and that made her feel bad, because none of this was Linc's fault. Maybe once they got back to Houston, she'd have her emotions under control. For now, she just needed to get through the day without falling apart.

The cab dropped them off on Rhode Island Avenue, in front of Cheryl's historic Victorian row house. As soon as they entered the foyer, they were swept up in a flurry of activity.

Cheryl had two kids, Angela, who was seven, and Benjamin, who was ten. Her husband, Ted, wasn't home, because as an HVAC specialist, he worked Saturdays. There were hugs and squeezes among Shelly and the three of them, until Cheryl looked to the doorway and saw Linc.

"Oh my God. Are you kidding me? He's here!" Cheryl shrieked. Then she shoved Shelly aside and rushed toward Linc, pulling him into an aggressive bear hug.

To his credit, he took it well, holding his *Time* magazine cover out to her. "Shelly asked me to bring this to you."

"Have mercy. You even autographed it for me!" Cheryl cried. Once again, Linc was pulled into an enthusiastic hug. "This is a wonderful surprise." Then Cheryl paused, looking back and forth between the two of them. "Obviously, the two of you were able to work out your differences. Is there something I should know?" she asked, wagging her brows up and down.

Since she'd started seeing Linc, Shelly had dropped out of contact with her sister. When she'd called to tell Cheryl that she was coming to visit, she hadn't mentioned that Linc would be with her. Now that it was time to explain her relationship with him, the words just wouldn't come.

Linc sidestepped over to Shelly and slipped his arm around her shoulders. "Don't start making wedding plans yet, but we're definitely getting along," he said, finishing the statement with a wink.

Shelly squirmed under Linc's arm. Wedding plans? Had he just given her sister the impression that they'd be headed down that road before long?

Feeling more uncomfortable by the minute, Shelly said, "We have so much to catch up on, Cheryl. I can't wait to sit down with you."

As if on cue, the kids started swirling around Linc's legs.

"I want to show you my room. My mom got me a model of the space station," announced Benjamin.

Angela, who was normally shy, perked up. "I want to show him my room first."

"I'm the oldest. I'll go first," declared Benjamin. "Besides, he's an astronaut. He doesn't want to see your dolls. He wants to see my space station."

"Don't worry, kids. I'm looking forward to seeing both your rooms—dolls, space station, everything," said Linc.

With that, the kids bounded up the stairs, with Linc in tow.

Cheryl led Shelly into the living room and sat beside her on the sofa. "We'll let the kids play with Linc for a while. Then, after we've had some time to chat, we'll go rescue him. It's not every day I have a famous astronaut in my house, and I'm going to take advantage of it."

Shelly nodded, dreading to tell her sister what she was really doing in town. Fortunately, Cheryl was so keyed up, she had yet to zero in on Shelly's mood.

"This is big news," said Cheryl. "It seems you took my advice and charmed the pants off him. You two have made miles of progress since we last talked about him."

"Don't jump to conclusions, Cheryl. We're nowhere near wedding bells."

"Uh-oh. Is the romance cooling already? I'm surprised, because he sure seems into you. Why would you bring him to meet me if things aren't working out?"

"Linc flew me here on an air force jet so I could talk to Sylvia. He came with me as a friend doing a favor."

"So I was wrong about the romantic vibe I was picking up between you?"

Shelly shifted, averting her gaze. "Not really. We've been seeing each other."

"And?"

"And it's been going fine. I just have a lot on my mind right now. I don't know if I'm in a good place to get serious about someone. At first, I thought he wouldn't want that, either. But all the signs are pointing toward him wanting more from this relationship."

"So why are you acting like that's a bad thing? He's one of the hottest men I've ever seen, and he's a bona fide hero. He's the stuff dreams are made of, and the crazy man wants *you*."

Shelly's heart started hammering in her chest, and her palms started sweating. This was all so much pressure.

"Calm down, Shelly. I see you starting to freak out. He made it clear that he's not on the verge of proposing, so chill out. Why don't you tell me why you needed to talk to Mom so urgently that you flew out here on an air force jet?"

Shelly closed her eyes for a moment to collect her

nerves. When she opened them, she launched into an explanation of what Linc had learned about her past three applications for the astronaut program.

Not wanting to lose momentum, despite Cheryl's horrified gasps and animated expression, Shelly didn't stop talking until she'd described her entire confrontation with their mother yesterday.

When her story was over, Cheryl slapped her thighs, shaking her head in outrage. "I honestly don't know why I'm surprised. But I am. I'm truly shocked."

Shelly felt her anger rising anew. "How am I supposed to ever forgive her? She's always been controlling, but this?"

Cheryl nodded. "Do you remember when I wanted to open my salon in a strip mall, and Mom kept encouraging me to go for a more upscale clientele? She kept sending in her bougie political friends, thinking that would force me to change my focus. I always knew that woman had a meddlesome streak, but this really is taking it to the extreme."

"I made her promise that she'd try to undo the damage she's done. But how can I trust her to keep her word? And even if she does, it may be too late."

"Is this the reason you've started pushing Linc away?" asked Cheryl.

Shelly frowned at her sister. That was the last thing she'd expected her to say. "What do you mean?"

"He was the messenger. You just found out that you can't trust the one person on earth who should always have your back. Now you're thinking, if you can't trust your own mother, how can you trust some man who has no reason to stand by you when times get rough?"

Shelly's skin prickled. She hated that she was so

transparent to her sister. Cheryl should have gone into psychology instead of hairdressing.

Wanting to avoid the issue, Shelly tried to gloss over her sister's words. "Look, none of this has anything to do with Linc. This is something I need to work out on my own."

Cheryl pinned her with one of her direct looks. "Just make sure that while you're soul searching, you don't ruin something that could be real. We don't get many chances at love. And from the way you're running, I'd say your feelings for Linc are stronger than you want to admit. Don't wait until it's too late to tell him how you feel."

Shelly had had enough. These heavy topics were weighing her down, and all she wanted to do was escape. "Don't worry about me. I'll figure it out. But while I'm here, can you give me a trim? I don't know if I'll survive any more Houston hair salons."

Shelly then went on to tell her all about her adventures in beauty since their last conversation. By the time Cheryl had finished reshaping her hair, Linc had returned with the kids. They all went out to a restaurant for dinner.

Shelly decided she would figure out her feelings for Linc later. For now, she was just going to enjoy visiting home.

Chapter 11

Linc pulled his car into the winding drive of his ranch. Stepping out of the car, Shelly took a deep breath of thick, muggy air and joked, "And to think I was starting to miss that good old Houston humidity."

She was trying her best to pull herself out of the emotional crater she'd been stuck in all weekend. She felt bad that she and Linc had barely spoken over the last two days. After all, none of her devastating revelations were his fault, despite the fact that they were inextricably linked to him.

In an effort to make up for her emotional distance, Shelly had agreed to spend the remainder of the weekend at Linc's house.

Despite all that had gone wrong in the last few days, she had one brilliant hope to cling to—she could still become an astronaut. None of those past rejections were her fault.

With her prior training and background, she truly believed the astronaut program would accept her now. That alone was reason enough to put her soggy mood behind her.

While Linc unpacked the car, Shelly wandered into the kitchen and was surprised to find Adelina there. Crossing the room, she walked happily into the older woman's embrace.

"What are you doing here, Adelina? I thought this was your day off."

Adelina's olive-skinned face warmed with her tiny laugh. "Day off, day on…I come when Lincoln needs me. My husband took the kids to watch baseball, so I came over to drop off some covered dishes. Since you're both here, I'll make you some homemade tamales for dinner."

Shelly tried to protest, but Adelina insisted that cooking for them would make her day. "You really spoil us, Adelina," Shelly said, moving to a stool to watch her pull fresh ingredients out of the refrigerator.

"And after you're married, I'll spoil your children, too." Her face lit with anticipation. "I can't wait for you and Lincoln to fill this house with babies."

Shelly's heart stopped. "Don't you think you're getting ahead of yourself? Linc and I aren't ready—"

Pulling on rubber gloves, Adelina started removing the stems and seeds from chili pods. "Don't worry. Lincoln has matured a lot since you came into his life. He's finally admitted that he would like to have a family."

Shelly's heart had restarted, but now it pounded at an erratic pace. "You mean 'one day,' don't you?"

Busy with her task, Adelina didn't look up to see that

Shelly's face had gone pale. "For years, I begged him to think about settling down with a family. He always told me that it would never happen. But suddenly he's changed. Now he says he would like to settle down. I think he knows you're the one. I knew as soon as I saw you."

Shelly knew Adelina thought she was being reassuring, but panic had come over Shelly so fast, she could barely breathe. Her mother's words were mingling with Adelina's and choking her thoughts. *Be a good mother. Start a family. Space is too dangerous.*

She gave the older woman a dim smile, jumping off the kitchen stool. "I'm going to go for a walk…or something."

"Take your time, honey," Adelina called after her. "The tamales won't be ready for another three hours."

Linc came out of his den and nearly bumped into Shelly, who was sleepwalking like a zombie. He reached out to steady her with his hands. "Are you all right?"

She nodded, but she didn't look all right. "Can we talk?"

"Sure," he said, leading her to the sofa in the living room. He tried not to get concerned as he sat next to her. Her mood had been much improved since they'd left D.C., and he thought she was finally shaking off her funk.

"You never told me what happened with your mom," he said, hoping that was what she wanted to discuss.

She shrugged. "My mother claims she wanted to protect me. Space is dangerous. Blah, blah, blah. Nothing she could have said would have satisfied me, anyway. But I made her promise to undo the damage she's done. We'll see if she keeps her promise."

Linc nodded. "Well, that's something. You'll probably get a fair shot at the astronaut program now. Feel free to use me as a reference. I'm certain that with your strong background, you won't have any more problems."

"We'll see." Shelly stared at the carpet. "Can I ask you a question?"

"Sure."

"Do you want to have kids?"

Linc smiled, picturing Shelly holding a newborn baby in her arms. "Definitely," he answered, without hesitation.

She nodded. "So, you're getting to the point when you're thinking of settling down?"

He took her hand. "I'm thinking about it. And you definitely factor into that thinking." He raised his gaze to hers and was surprised to see complete terror in her eyes.

She pulled her hand out of his. "I'm not ready for all of that, Linc. I don't think I'm in the right head space to focus on a relationship right now."

"Shelly, I'm not saying we have to get married and start a family right now. There's plenty of time for that."

She shifted away from him. "I really can't do this. It's not fair to you, because I don't know when, if ever, I'll be ready for those things."

Where had he heard that before? From Shelly's own mouth. She'd broken up with her last boyfriend for the same reasons. Linc refused to believe that things weren't different for them.

"You don't have to run away. It would be one thing if I believed for a second that you weren't starting to have real feelings for me. You're the first person since I was a teenager that I let myself fall in love with."

Shelly's body went still. "You're in love with me?"

"Of course. I knew when we got together that you weren't the type of woman that men got bored with. You're sassy and you're fun. And you can be really sweet when you want to be. How could I not fall for you?"

Tears started rolling down her cheeks. "It would have been so much easier if I could have continued to think of you as a pretty-boy player. Someone who doesn't care about relationships because the next one will be along in fifteen minutes."

Linc's heart hammered in his chest. "What would be easier?"

"Telling you the truth. I just don't think I can give you what you want. My career is everything to me. Now that I know I'm finally going to have a shot at my dream—that all those failures in the past weren't my fault—I can't let anything steal my focus."

"I'm not trying to steal your focus. I just want to love you. Why can't you have your career *and* me?"

Shelly wiped her face with her hands. "Linc, you're not the kind of man a girl takes in small doses. You're the hot fudge sundae—one bite and you want the whole thing. If I let myself fall for you, I could really lose myself. And the worst thing about that is I probably wouldn't mind it a bit."

"You're making this more difficult than it has to be. We can work together. The last two weeks have proven that—"

"This is my decision, and I can't afford to change my mind. If you press me, you could probably talk me out of it, because I really do care about you. But please don't. I'll only resent you for it later."

Linc's entire body went cold. Her decision was final. She didn't want him. Was he going to continue to sit there and beg her to love him after he'd just put his heart on the line for her?

He came to his feet. "Fine. If this is what you really want. Then that's the end of it." Linc got halfway to the foyer; then he turned around.

"Adelina is constantly warning me about getting too comfortable on my own," he said in a low voice. "She said one day I'd wake up alone and regret it. It took a while, but I finally realized that she was right. I hope you don't have to learn that lesson the hard way."

Shelly took a cab home from Linc's ranch. It wasn't until she was safe inside her four walls that she let herself crumble. "I know I did the right thing," she repeated over and over again.

It had to be the right thing, despite how miserable it made her. Two days ago, she'd felt like the biggest sucker in the world. Here a huge government conspiracy had been going on right under her nose, and she'd had no clue. She'd just blindly believed what she'd been told.

After that shocking wake-up call, she'd discovered that her mother had selfishly denied her the one thing she'd always wanted above all else.

How long was she going to go on being a sucker? Linc was a wonderful man, but he was too intoxicating. He was like a drug she couldn't get enough of. She'd blink her eyes, and she'd be married and pregnant, with her dream of being an astronaut drifting away forever.

Still, it had broken her heart to walk away. He'd told her he loved her. For one fleeting second, she'd wanted to rejoice in that admission. She, Shelly London, had stolen the heart of one of America's most eligible bachelors. A man who dated starlets and models. She was the one who'd finally made him fall.

A ragged sob broke free of her lungs. There wasn't any celebrating to be done. She'd just broken his heart. It wasn't lost on her what a difficult thing it must have been for him to tell her his feelings. To put his heart in harm's way for her. How she was going to live with causing him that kind of heartache, she just didn't know.

But it was better that they both made this sacrifice now. Before the relationship went too far. He'd medicate himself with bar outings with his friends and all the female attention he could stand.

That thought brought a stab of pain to her chest. She hated the thought of Linc with another woman. But she couldn't have it both ways. She'd decided to put herself first.

She was going to have to live with that decision.

Seeing Linc at work was more painful than Shelly had anticipated. It would have been easier if he'd taken their split badly and ignored her or reverted to his initial adversarial position.

Instead, he always waved or gave her a smile that, she occasionally saw, was tinged with pain. They were polite in each other's presence, but they kept as safe a distance as possible from each other.

Shelly helped the team make crucial adjustments in the Neutral Buoyancy Lab, and training whizzed by. Finally, they had reached the moment they'd all been waiting for: flight testing, the most crucial of all their prelaunch preparations.

The deadline for the mission was approaching

swiftly. Guardian's orbit was degrading fast, and they were running out of time. The entire team moved to Edwards Air Force Base in the Mojave Desert to observe the flight tests.

After a couple of weeks without incident, everyone assumed the new security measures were working. They were certain that there wouldn't be any further accidents during training. But those hopes proved to be short-lived.

Before Draco's first air launch, it was discovered that someone had hacked into the spacecraft's computer system. It was a critical discovery as the hacking could have caused the spacecraft to crash before the crew could take over control.

The subtle programming change that would have ended the entire mission was caught by a fluke. One of the techs just happened to notice that Draco's computer code file was slightly larger than it should be. He reviewed it line by line and discovered an important discrepancy.

This news rocked the entire team. But no one as much as Shelly. She'd come within inches of watching Linc die in a fiery crash for the second time.

Again, Shelly questioned her decision to break things off with Linc. What if he died in that spacecraft? What if Draco went into space and didn't return?

At least she could have had these last few weeks of memories with him.

Shocked by her emotions, Shelly wasn't sure she could watch the flight testing once the repairs were made to the computer system. Although security was ramped up yet again, she couldn't stop fearing the worst.

Now, as Shelly sat in the control booth, her palms

began to sweat. Linc, Vince and Paul were in the space-craft, and the B-52 was preparing for takeoff. It would fly high enough to initiate the air launch; then Linc would invert Draco, fly in a circle and land.

Everything on Draco and the B-52 had been checked and rechecked. The spacecraft had been cleared for testing, but Shelly couldn't shake the gnawing fear inside her. As the B-52 took off successfully, her chest constricted. Instead of feeling relieved, she felt as if she could barely breathe.

Starting to take deeper and deeper breaths, Shelly tried to force enough air into her lungs. The pain in her chest went from tight to stabbing.

She felt a bead of sweat trickle down to her temple as she studied the monitor. Linc was going to die. She was about to watch him die.

Thankfully, everyone else in the control booth was too focused on the activity going on to notice Shelly's panic. She considered getting up and leaving the control booth before launch separation, but she knew her shaky knees wouldn't hold her up.

So, she was forced to watch Linc and the other as-tronauts, feeling for all the world as though she were about to have a heart attack.

As the pyros fired, Shelly held her breath, visualiz-ing an explosion in her mind's eye. Instead, Draco detached from the B-52 safely, and her head began to swim.

She could barely focus on the remainder of the exercise for the whirring in her skull and the need to constantly remind her brain to force air through her constricted lungs.

When Linc and the other astronauts were finally on

the ground and disembarking from the spacecraft, Shelly went almost numb with relief.

How on earth would she survive the real thing if she could barely stand to watch the flight test? She was instantly hit with the overwhelming need to protect Linc.

For a fleeting moment, a crazy thought popped into her head. If she sabotaged the mission herself, Linc would have to stay on the ground.

As that thought entered and left her mind, she suddenly understood her mother a little better. When you cared about someone enough, you wanted to do irrational things to keep them out of harm's way.

Of course, Shelly never would act on her impulsive thought, but her mother had always been a woman of action. If something bothered her, she made it go away. Period.

When Shelly got back to her hotel room that evening, she decided to call her mother. She didn't know what she wanted to say. Her newfound perspective didn't excuse her mother's actions. But her estrangement from Linc was harder than she'd counted on, and she didn't want to lose contact with her mother, too.

Sylvia answered her cell phone on the second ring. "Hello?"

"Hi. It's Shelly."

"Shelly, I'm glad to hear from you. If you're calling to find out if I've made good on my promise, I have good news. NASA is considering your application for next year's astronaut candidate class. Most likely you'll be hearing from the program soon."

Shelly's heart jumped in her chest. "That's fantastic news, but that's not why I called. We had such a contentious conversation last time we spoke. I wanted to make sure I told you that I love you. And I forgive you for what you did. I don't expect anything like this to happen again, but I think I understand why you did it."

Her mother's voice was breathy. "Shelly, you don't know how happy I am to hear you say that. I never wanted to hurt you. Quite the opposite."

"I know."

"But I realize you're not my little girl to protect anymore. You've been a grown woman for some time. One I can be proud of. Both you and your sister turned out so well. Sometimes I wonder if that's because of me or despite me."

Shelly laughed. "Both. I've got some of your best and your worst traits. But I wouldn't trade them for anything."

When she finally hung up with her mother, she was feeling a lot better. But now that she wasn't seeing Linc anymore, she felt isolated again.

Most of the time the training was so hectic, there wasn't time to dwell on that. But at times like these, when she was alone at night, she felt the isolation.

Linc was out there somewhere, not too far away. She couldn't help wondering what he was doing. Was he alone? Her heartbeat sped up. Was he with someone?

Shelly forced herself to ignore the stabbing pain in her heart. She'd given up the right to worry about Linc's whereabouts.

She just needed to ride out this pain. It would go away eventually, wouldn't it?

Linc chugged his beer and then slammed the glass on the table. "I still think this place doesn't compare to Boondoggles," he said to his fellow astronauts.

Vince shook his head. "Boondoggles is a dive."

"The best dive in the world," Paul chimed in. "It has great pizza and cheap beer."

"Plus, they treat us like we're royalty," Linc added.

Paul gave Linc a high five. "What more could you ask for?"

The three of them were in a small California bar, not far from the flight testing site. For the past few weeks, Linc had been turning down offers to hang out with his crew, but he'd known that was going to have to change.

The mission was drawing close, and he needed bonding time with the guys. He also needed to start *acting* like his old self until he began to *feel* like his old self again. Shelly wasn't going to change her mind, and pining after her only made him feel like a lovesick puppy.

Vince tapped his fingers on the hardwood table. "It won't be long now. I can't wait to get up there," he said, referring to their mission.

Paul snorted. "Of course, you can't wait. The two of you have to maneuver the spacecraft. I have the *real* dirty work."

Vince shrugged. "Dude, we're all in this together. You screw up your job, and you take us with you."

Linc slammed his beer on the table harder than he'd intended. "That's not going to happen."

Both men gave him odd looks. "Of course not," they both replied at once.

Linc knew he was a bit more on edge than usual. But he couldn't let that get in the way of his mission. He'd been reviewing the flight protocols over and over, and he'd put in extra training time whenever he could.

Security was tighter than ever. Despite the problems

that had occurred in the past, everything was going to go according to plan on launch day.

He repeated this to himself daily, but he still wasn't convinced. Falling in love with Shelly had thrown him off his game in more ways than one.

Even though they weren't seeing each other anymore, he was still battling a very real fear that he'd never see her again.

This was exactly the reason he'd avoided long-term attachments in the past. No one to whine about his safe return, and no one to distract him from his job.

But there was nothing he could do about his feelings for Shelly. Maybe they'd fade on their own; maybe they wouldn't. He still had a job to do, and he had to put away these nagging fears and just get it done.

Vince shook Linc's elbow. "What's gotten into you, man? You really haven't been yourself lately."

Paul nodded. "Yeah. Is the stress getting to you? These accidents?"

"No, I'm fine. I was having some girl trouble, but none of that matters now," replied Linc.

Vince's eyes went wide. "Girl trouble? You? I never thought I'd see the day. Who was it? Another model?"

"Nope. I think that was my problem," Linc confessed. "I should have stuck to the models. They're less complicated. Higher maintenance, but they don't concern themselves with deeper issues. At least not the ones I've dated."

Paul laughed at him. "Wait till I tell my girlfriend how the mighty have fallen. What made you break it off? Was she jealous?"

Linc grunted. He didn't know why he was spilling his guts, but it felt good to get it off his chest. "She dumped me."

"No way!" Both men erupted into peals of laughter.

Linc sighed. "Thanks for mocking my pain."

When the laughter died down, Vince paused, studying Linc's face. "Oh, jeez, you were serious about this girl."

"I was. And I still am," said Linc.

"It must be karma," Paul said, laughing, and Vince punched him in the arm.

"Seriously, man. Is there any chance of making it work with this girl?" asked Vince.

Linc shrugged. "She has a lot of pride, and she's pretty strong willed. But the upside is that I really think she's fighting her feelings for me by staying away. She thinks I'll derail her career."

Paul blinked hard, realization coming to his eyes. "Oh my God. Is it Shelly?"

Linc released a vicious curse. "If she finds out I told anyone on the mission about us, she'd never speak to me again."

Vince looked at him solemnly. "I've got bigger secrets than this one under my belt. You don't have to worry about me," he said, turning to look at Paul.

"What? I'm not trustworthy?" said Paul. "Of course, I'll keep it to myself. But I should have known. There were sparks flying between the two of you from day one."

Vince nodded. "Now that I think about it, she's perfect for you. She won't put up with any of your bull. A guy with your ego needs someone to keep him in check."

"Thanks a lot," Linc grumbled. But it lifted his spirits to hear that his colleagues thought he and Shelly were a match. Maybe when the mission was over…

Paul slapped the table. "Screw her career. Go and get that, my man!"

Linc shook his head. "I wish it were that easy."

* * *

The next morning, when Shelly arrived at the flight testing site, she was given a message to report to Colonel Murphy. Not wanting to keep him waiting, she went straight to his temporary office on Edwards Air Force Base.

As soon as Shelly walked into the room, all eyes turned on her. In addition to Colonel Murphy, all of GRM's astronauts and several military officials she didn't recognize were there.

Colonel Murphy's eyes were hard with accusation. "There's been another security breach."

Before Shelly could formulate a response, a newspaper was thrust into her hands.

"Shelly, do you know anything about this?" asked the colonel.

Startled, Shelly looked down at the newspaper. The headline read Secret Government Spacecraft Plagued By Accidents.

Chapter 12

Shelly's entire body went hot. "How did this get in the newspaper?"

"That's what we'd like to know," said one of the unnamed suits in the room.

Shelly swallowed hard, pushing down the acid making its way up from her stomach. They were all looking at her. They all thought she had something to do with this.

Only Linc's gaze was sympathetic. The other two astronauts kept their eyes averted.

"If you're asking if I'm responsible for this, the answer is no. I haven't spoken to anyone," Shelly said in her defense.

"It's interesting that the leak didn't occur until after your security clearance was upgraded." It was the unidentified suit again.

"Since you're so clearly accusing me of something, may I at least have your name?" asked Shelly.

"Albert Yates, secretary of defense," he said smugly.

Shelly felt her spine grow cold. "Well, I wish I could say it's a pleasure to meet you, but I haven't lied to you yet, and I'm not about to start."

There were several startled intakes of breath in the room, but Shelly knew that if she showed fear or reverence, they'd have her at a disadvantage.

"I don't know anything about this story getting leaked to the newspaper," she continued. "I haven't had the time to so much as *read* a newspaper, let alone speak to one. If you hadn't given me this one, I still wouldn't know about any of this."

Secretary Yates advanced on her, standing inches from her nose. "That's a very convenient answer. And, quite frankly, I wouldn't have expected you to say anything else. After all, if you *were* the responsible party, you certainly wouldn't admit it under these circumstances."

Shelly had the feeling that he was threatening to torture her. She opened her mouth to speak, and his pointed finger in her face shut her up. He narrowed his eyes at her, and she resisted the urge to back up. *Show no weakness*, she cautioned herself.

"If you look around this room, Ms. London, you'll see that one of these things is not like the other. That thing is you," said Secretary Yates. "You're the only person here whose security clearance was upgraded in the last few weeks. I'd say the timing coincides suspiciously with this information leak."

It was Shelly's turn to narrow her eyes. "It's my understanding, *Mr. Secretary*—" she was sure to say his name as mockingly as he'd said hers "—that you were the one to approve that security upgrade for me. You're not suddenly implying that you made a mistake, are you?"

Secretary Yates's face turned beet-red, his mouth opening and closing as he struggled for the words to properly eviscerate her.

Shelly felt her face reddening as well. Now even *she* couldn't believe her own nerve. Antagonizing one of the most powerful men in the country was not a prudent career move.

"Let's not get off track here," Colonel Murphy interjected. "Shelly, I think the appropriate action for us to take right now is to reassign you to another project. Training is almost complete, and I'm certain your staff can fill in for the interim. That will give us time to determine the source of this leak."

Shelly's jaw dropped. "Is that how things work around here? Guilty until proven innocent? Why do I have to be the scapegoat when I've done nothing wrong?"

"Shelly, this isn't an indictment," said the colonel. "It's just a precautionary measure. Secretary Yates feels strongly that—"

"May I say something here?" Linc took a step forward. Shelly had almost forgotten he was in the room.

"Commander Ripley," Secretary Yates began.

"With all due respect, Mr. Secretary, you gathered us all in here to discuss this issue. I think there should actually be some discussion before any decisions are made," said Linc.

"What's on your mind, Ripley?" the colonel asked.

"Colonel Murphy, I encouraged you to upgrade Shelly's security clearance, and I take full responsibility for that decision," replied Linc.

Shelly held her breath, hearing Linc's stern tone. It gave her a secret thrill that he wanted to stand up for her. But she didn't know what he could possibly say to help her now.

"Shelly London has been tireless in her dedication to this mission," Linc continued. "If you're going to hold her responsible for this press leak, then you might as well hold her responsible for the fire on Draco's simulator and the hacking into Draco's computer system. And I think you know as well as I do, that would be ridiculous."

"I don't know—" Secretary Yates began, but Linc interrupted him.

"She designed Draco herself. Why would she destroy her own creation? Seeing this craft launched into space is her dream come true. But if *that* logic doesn't convince you, what about the fact that there's been a formal investigation into these incidents of sabotage and no one has identified Shelly London as a suspect? In fact, to the best of my knowledge, no one has been targeted on this team. Secretary Yates is here because Washington wants someone's head on a platter, and since Shelly is the most expendable, you've chosen her."

"Now wait a minute," Secretary Yates stormed.

Linc went on. "If this is how this investigation is going to be run—we have no real suspects, so let's invent one—then you can have my resignation right now. I stand behind Shelly's integrity. I want to get on with this mission, but if you're going to sacrifice her to appease the bureaucracy, then you can count me out. Good luck finding another pilot to lead this team."

Vince stepped forward, next to Linc. "I'm with Lightning. I'd stake my career on the fact that no one in this room is responsible for the security breaches, and if we can't see this mission through together, then I'm out, too."

Paul joined his two crew members. "Ditto."

The room erupted into chatter, and no one could be heard over anyone else.

Shelly watched this scene unfolding with disbelief. Her heart was so warm, it was all she could do to keep the tears from falling out of her eyes. She'd never expected this kind of loyalty. Especially after all she'd been through with Linc.

Colonel Murphy started waving his hands to calm the commotion of everyone talking at once. "All right, all right. This is getting out of hand. You've heard from your mission team, Secretary Yates. How do you want to proceed?"

Still red-faced, Secretary Yates surveyed the room, clearly looking for a way out of this corner. "Fine," he said tightly. "The team will remain as is for the time being. But I'll be watching all of you. From now on, every testing site is going to have armed military guards on post. And there will be daily reports sent directly to me."

Secretary Yates left the room abruptly, hastily followed by his subordinates from Washington. And, after they vacated the room, everyone fell silent. Then they suddenly burst into celebratory applause and exchanged congratulations and sighs of relief.

Shelly went to each of the astronauts and thanked them profusely. When she stopped in front of Linc, her throat went dry.

"I don't know if I even have the words to properly thank you for what you did for me today," she told him.

He waved her off. "Then don't thank me. I was just standing up for what I believe in. It could have been any one of us with our neck on the chopping block. The mission is at a critical stage, and none of us is expendable. We can't let anyone be sacrificed without real or even circumstantial evidence weighing against them."

Even though he made it sound impersonal—after all, they did have a large audience—Shelly knew his act was, in fact, very personal. And she wasn't sure how to handle that knowledge.

Colonel Murphy didn't let the fanfare go on long, dismissing them all and ordering them to return to work. But Shelly remained fixated on the incident throughout the day.

Lincoln Ripley had put his illustrious and highly decorated career on the line for her today. She couldn't say she would have done the same for him.

She'd spent weeks convincing him that nothing was more important than her career goals, and here he had endangered his future for a lot less than their shot at love.

Sure, she could rationalize that his job had never really been in jeopardy. NASA simply couldn't afford to lose their only remaining mission commander. Still, they couldn't make him fly without his consent, and in that instant, she had fully believed he was prepared to walk away.

She should have been happy. She'd narrowly escaped that room with her job intact. Instead, she felt sick to her stomach.

Linc had demonstrated his true feelings for her in a way she hadn't been able to do. Did she love him? It was a thought she'd ardently avoided.

No matter how fast she ran from her feelings, they seemed to be gaining on her. When they finally caught up to her, Shelly didn't know what she'd do.

It seemed all the complications she'd hoped to avoid by breaking things off with Linc had arisen, anyway.

Had she condemned herself to be alone for no reason?

Several days later, flight testing was successfully completed, and Draco was moved to Johnson Space Center for final diagnostic testing.

It was Saturday, and probably Linc's last day off before the mission. Tomorrow Draco would be packed up and moved to the launch site in Florida, and Linc would soon be back in space.

He was gearing up for the most exciting time of the entire endeavor, the actual mission, and for once, it left him cold.

He'd offered to give it all up for her, without any hope of getting any of the things he needed from her in return. It was official. He had it bad. He hadn't been in love with Shelly for very long, and he'd been convinced that this fact would make his lovesickness easier to cure.

But the reality was that these feelings weren't going away. They only grew stronger. Each day he didn't see her, her face floated in his dreams. Every time he had a personal victory, she was the only person he wanted to tell.

And when she stared down the secretary of defense himself and dared him to admit he'd made a mistake, Linc had felt an overwhelming sense of pride. Despite the fact that it might have been the most reckless thing he'd ever seen her do.

He would have walked away from GRM without any regrets, but he'd also felt in his gut that he could save her. Making an example of Shelly had outraged him, and he wouldn't have tolerated it even if he'd been powerless to change her fate.

Yet, he hadn't expected his boys to stand by him. It had been a turning point for everyone in that room. They'd all been through too much together to sell each other out. And that knowledge was the only glue holding him together now.

Collecting the group's beer steins, Linc headed back to their table at Boondoggles and set the beers down in front of Vince and Paul. "What are you guys talking about?"

"About what a punk you've become lately," Paul answered.

Linc's head snapped back. "Excuse me?"

Paul nudged Vince. "See, I told you there's still some fight left in him."

Linc squared his shoulders. "Are you going to tell me what the hell you're talking about, or is there going to be a bar fight?"

"Now you're talking," Paul said.

Vince punched Paul in the arm. "Stop riling him up." Then he said to Linc, "We just think you're fighting a losing battle. Breakups are tough, but we're afraid this one could affect our mission."

"I didn't ask you all to back me up in Colonel Murphy's office," Linc said, bristling.

Vince shook his head. "That's not what we're talking about. They were trying to shaft her. You were right to stand up to them. I know you would have done the same for either of us."

Linc relaxed. "Then what's the problem?"

"Your head's not in the game," Paul said. "You've lost your edge."

If Linc hadn't just been thinking something very similar, he would have taken offense. As it was, all he could do was stare at his two fellow crew members.

"You're Lightning Ripley, commander of this spacecraft," Vince reminded him. "You've never been the kind of guy to let a girl get in his head. Especially when there's so much at stake."

Paul joined in. "That's right. Shelly's a great girl, but she's hardly the only girl. The only reason you're hung up on her is that she's first girl to finally turn you down."

"She'll probably realize her mistake eventually, but if she never does, it's her loss. Either way, you've got to shake it off," Vince said.

Linc watched his two friends. Their faces were etched with concern. It wasn't just because they were about to be launched into space on an experimental craft and were depending on him for their safe return. He could see they really cared. They wouldn't have stood up with him in Colonel Murphy's office if they didn't respect him.

What was he letting himself become? "I'm sorry if I let my emotions get a hold on me. I've never really been in love before. I didn't know it was this hard," Linc confessed.

"Man, love sucks," Paul said vehemently. He was quiet for a moment. "Don't tell my girlfriend I said that."

Vince sighed. "I've been married twelve years, and it's definitely not easy. But it's worth it."

"Yeah? You think so?" asked Linc.

Vince nodded. "When we get back, you have two choices. If you think Shelly loves you, don't let anything stand between you and her. If you think she doesn't, move on. You can have any woman you want. I hate you for it. But it's true."

Paul shrugged. "If going into space isn't the ultimate distraction from a broken heart, I don't know what is."

A slow smile crept across Linc's lips. Suddenly, he was feeling better than he had in a long time. How could he let a woman, even one that made him feel the way Shelly did, get in the way of the job?

What would he be doing right now if he hadn't let his emotions jump into the driver's seat? He'd be focused on the mission. And with the recent problems with security, he'd probably be looking over Draco himself, one last time before it was shipped to Cape Canaveral.

Linc pushed aside the beer, which he'd barely touched. "Anyone want to visit the spacecraft with me?"

Vince jumped up. "Now there's the man I know. I'm in."

Paul didn't move, shaking his head pitifully. "I can't. My girlfriend's meeting me here. If I don't spend every available moment with her before launch, she's threatened to dump me."

Linc and Vince both rolled their eyes and headed out the door.

Shelly pulled up in front of building 5. Right now it was the most secure building on the Johnson campus. There were two armed military guards posted at the only key-card entrance. All the other doors had been temporarily sealed while Draco was being housed there.

Turning off her engine, Shelly noted that she had exactly thirty-five minutes before the building would be sealed off entirely for the night. First thing Sunday morning, a crew would be in to box up Draco and ship it to the launch site in Florida.

She would have shown up sooner, but she'd decided to try her luck at another hair salon. The dry desert heat had made her complacent. As soon as she'd returned to Houston's humidity, her hair had shriveled up enough to rival an Afro.

Right now, her hair was slicked up in a tight French roll, with light side bangs. Her stylist, Janet, had assured her it would hold up through a category five hurricane. Shelly just wished that was all the stylist had said to her.

She didn't know what had been in those hair chemicals, but they'd somehow loosened her lips, and Shelly had found herself spilling out her heartache to the older woman.

Janet had been kind and a good listener, but the trouble had come when she'd started doling out advice. She'd been blunt and unapologetic with her opinions.

Her words still echoed in Shelly's head. *You're a fool if you let anything stand between you and love. We can't wish on the future. All we're guaranteed is right now.*

"Damn you, Janet, and your wisdom," Shelly muttered as she got out of the car. The timing was all wrong for her to start reevaluating her relationship with Linc. For now, she had to live with the way things were.

The problem was that Shelly could barely sleep at night, worrying over this mission. The investigation still hadn't pinpointed a real suspect. She couldn't keep Linc out of space, the way her mother had tried to keep her out. But she could do everything in her power to make sure Linc returned to Earth safely.

That was why she had to look over the spacecraft one last time. She'd be there to confirm for herself that when the building was locked down at 6:00 p.m., Draco was exactly as it should be.

Shelly walked up to the guards and signed in, then used her key card to enter the building. She knew she'd find Draco in the high bay, which was basically an enormous garage. What she didn't expect to find was Linc and Vince already in the room.

Both men turned as she approached.

"I didn't expect to find you guys here," Shelly said. And she hadn't expected the jolt to her heart at the sight of Linc.

He reached out and touched Draco's hull. "This is my spacecraft. I wanted to see for myself that everything was in place."

Shelly tried not to bristle at his show of ownership. But he knew how to push her buttons. "There are armed guards at the doors. Why wouldn't everything be in place?"

Linc's wicked grin had returned. "If you have so much faith in the system, what are *you* doing here?"

"I just needed to… I had to check the… I'm here for the same reason," she said, with a heavy sigh. There was so much she wished she could say. But this wasn't the time or place, and they had an audience. "Are you guys almost finished?"

Linc narrowed his eyes. "What? We can't even occupy the same space now? You have to face it, Shelly. Training is over. You have to let go. This baby's in my care now."

She felt her body go hot. Why was he taking that tone with her? "I designed Draco from its first bolt. It will always be *my* baby."

Linc laughed mirthlessly. "I see that your mother passed her controlling streak on to you."

Shelly gasped. The conversation had a very familiar feel. Clearly, his feelings for her had gone, enabling him to take such a cheap shot. Now they were back at square one—bickering opponents.

Vince started backing toward the door. "I've seen what I came to see. I'll wait for you in the car, Lightning."

Shelly and Linc were silent until the door slammed shut.

"Okay. For the record, taking every precaution to make sure you don't die in a fiery explosion on launch day is *not* controlling," declared Shelly. "It's thorough. And while I may have gotten many traits from my mother, good and bad, I'm nothing like her."

"Really?" Linc asked. "Didn't you once tell me that you thought your parents divorced because your mother worked too hard?"

Shelly pressed her lips together tightly, not wanting to admit that this was true. "So?"

"So, aren't you on the verge of the very same thing? Sure, your mother eventually remarried, so maybe you're hoping that when you finally have what you want, someone will just show up for you. And, hey, maybe he will."

Shelly's heart hammered in her chest as she registered the intensity behind Linc's eyes. She'd never wanted to see him looking at her like this.

"But I can promise you," he continued emphatically, "you'll spend a lot of time wishing he was me."

With that, Linc turned on his heel and walked out, leaving Shelly trembling.

Shaken, she didn't move for several seconds. Then,

mechanically, she looked down at her watch. It was 5:55. Someone would be along any minute to lock down the room.

She'd better get to her inspection quickly. "This is your last chance to look over the spacecraft," she reminded herself aloud so it would register. Her head turned involuntarily toward the door. This was her last chance to see Linc.

She'd go to Cape Canaveral to watch the launch, but not until the actual day of the launch. All her duties involving Linc were over. For the next several days, he'd be completely immersed in astronaut activity.

Shelly looked back at Draco. Linc and Vince had already given it a once-over. It would be inspected again when it was assembled at Kennedy Space Center.

Linc had been right. She had to let go.

But not of him. She couldn't leave things this way. Not when he'd be going into space and this could be their last conversation.

All she was guaranteed was right now, Shelly thought, remembering Janet's words.

Rushing to the door, Shelly headed down the corridor at a brisk walk. She wanted to run, but she didn't want to look suspicious to the guards who would be coming in for the lockdown any minute.

She just hoped she could catch Linc in the parking lot before he drove off. If she didn't catch him, she reassured herself, she'd just have to stake out his house.

Suddenly, she couldn't bear to go another day without telling Linc how she felt. He might reject her. She wouldn't blame him if he did, but she wasn't going to run away from herself anymore.

Shelly was so caught up in her newfound self-awareness

that it took her a moment to register that there were voices coming from around the corner. One of them was Linc's.

And the other one…

Instinct brought her to a stop before she would have come into view. Although Linc's voice was calm, his words were anything but.

"You don't have to do this. Whatever trouble you're in, we can find a way out. Put the gun down before the guards show up."

"The guards aren't coming. I gassed them on the way in. And don't look for Vince, either. I took care of him, too." The voice was familiar. "I looked up to you. I actually really like you. That's why it's going to be so hard to shoot you. But I don't have a choice."

Shelly peered around the corner and saw the back of Quincy's head. He was holding a gun on Linc.

Chapter 13

Quincy was holding a gun on Linc? Shelly's rational mind almost wouldn't accept it. But the fact that Linc was in danger registered with brutal clarity.

If she didn't act fast, Linc would be shot.

She couldn't get help. Quincy had claimed to have gassed the military guards posted at the door. She believed him because his gun looked like one of their rifles. She didn't know what he'd done to Vince, but there wasn't time to dwell on that now.

Her mind went numb with panic. What should she do?

Linc was still talking to Quincy in a calm voice. "I know you wouldn't be doing this if you weren't in a lot of trouble. You're not a killer. Don't become one now."

Quincy, on the other hand, was near hysteria. "I never meant for this to happen. You're my hero. But they were going to kill me if I didn't get them their money."

"What money? Who was going to kill you?" Linc asked calmly.

Shelly listened with horror as Quincy told Linc about gambling debts and unnamed people who had offered to bail him out if Draco never got into space.

Part of her wanted to join the conversation and ask Quincy what on earth he thought he was doing. They'd been friends for years. He might confide in her.

She dismissed that idea. Then she and Linc would *both* be in danger. She'd lose the advantage of surprise.

Shelly forced her mind to focus as adrenaline coursed through her. Limbs trembling with energy, she ordered her body to move.

She backed away from the corner and began searching for a potential weapon. As dangerous as Quincy was with a rifle in his hand, he was unfocused and distracted. As long as Linc kept him talking, she had a chance. She could sneak up on him if she was fast enough.

Her gaze honed in on a metal toolbox on one of the tables against the wall. As quietly as possible, Shelly dug a heavy wrench out of the toolbox and tiptoed back to the corner. Her heart thundered in her ears so loudly, she feared it would give her away.

She was so scared, her arms were trembling as she crept around the corner. Without taking time to think, she raised the wrench over her head and let it fall solidly against Quincy's neck and shoulder.

Grunting in pain, Quincy went to his knees, and Linc snatched the rifle away from him. Startled that Quincy was still moving, she hit him again and again, until he passed out.

She dropped the wrench, staring at Quincy's body in

horror. Her panic spiked again. "Oh, no! I didn't kill him, did I?"

Linc's fingers probed Quincy's neck for a pulse. "No, he still has a heartbeat."

"Thank God," she said, gasping for air. Suddenly her entire body felt weak. Unable to contain herself, she fell into Linc's arms.

He squeezed her tight. "You saved my life."

"I was coming to tell you that I love you."

She felt his breath on her ear. "I couldn't have asked for better timing."

Shelly was still in bed when her doorbell started ringing Sunday afternoon. It had been a restless night. Her dreams had been plagued with images of Quincy, Linc and guns.

Part of her had been hoping it would all prove to be a horrible nightmare in the morning. Yet, when she'd opened her eyes to the sunlight streaming through her window, she'd had to face reality. Yesterday's events had been real.

Her head was hardly clear, but she couldn't ignore the persistent doorbell. Throwing a bathrobe over her shorts and tank, she rushed to the front door and peeked out.

She unlocked the door and pulled it open. "Linc? What's going on?"

"Can I come in?" He looked like a slice of heaven, standing on her shaded porch, with the glistening afternoon sun behind him.

Shelly reached up to touch her hair, expecting to feel wild bed head. Instead, she found her hair neatly bound in Janet's French roll, despite her restless flailing through the night.

Stepping back, Shelly opened the door wide. "Of course."

Remembering Vince, a shaft of worry jabbed her chest. After the authorities had arrived yesterday to collect Quincy, Vince had been found unconscious and stuffed into a closet. He'd been bleeding from a head wound.

"Is this about Vince?" Shelly asked. "You're not here to tell me that he's—"

"No, no. Vince is in stable condition. He has a pretty bad concussion, but he's awake."

Shelly clutched her chest. "He's not going to be able to fly, is he?"

Linc shook his head, taking a seat on her sofa. "Unfortunately not."

She sighed, sitting down next to him. "With Guardian's orbit rapidly degrading, they can't scrap the mission. But now we're a man down. I guess Quincy's plan worked out, after all."

She'd been able to get the rest of the story last night, when Quincy was taken into custody. Shelly and her engineering team, including Quincy, worked for Welloney, a contractor to NASA. Unbeknownst to the team, Lockwood, a rival contractor, had also been given the go-ahead to build a spacecraft for GRM, as a backup.

Quincy, who had never revealed to Shelly that he had an expensive gambling habit, had been paid off by a Lockwood executive to bump Welloney's spacecraft, Draco, from the mission. Then Lockwood could take over the GRM contract.

Despite Draco and its astronauts' recurring accidents, Welloney's team was never bumped from the mission, because Shelly's spacecraft design had been superior to Lockwood's.

But with only two astronauts trained to operate Draco, Shelly didn't see how her spacecraft was going to make it into space now.

"Quincy's plan *didn't* work, Shelly. Since he and a Lockwood employee were complicit in sabotaging the project, NASA has no interest in flying Lockwood's spacecraft. Not to mention the fact that Draco is the best fit for the job."

Shelly sank back into the sofa cushions, tucking her feet beneath her. "That's great to hear, but I just don't know how they'll pull the mission off."

He leaned toward her, his eyes dancing with excitement. "That's what I came to talk to you about. We think we found a way to continue the mission."

If NASA wanted to continue the mission, then Linc would still be going into space in a few days. Mixed emotions began warring in her head.

"It's not ideal," she said, trying to keep up with the conversation despite her growing distraction. "But I suppose, worst-case scenario, Draco could be manned by two people."

"No, it's going to be a three-person team. We've chosen—"

Shelly held up her hand to stop him. "Before you continue, can I say something?"

It didn't really matter who the third person would be. Right now the only thing she could think about was the possibility of losing him. She just couldn't let another moment pass without saying what was in her heart.

"Sure, but, Shelly, you're going to want to hear this first. It's about your career—"

"That's what I wanted to say. I was wrong to put my

career ahead of our relationship. I think I was just scared. But I've finally figured out that dreams are meaningless if you're all alone. If I got everything I wanted tomorrow, I still wouldn't be happy unless I had you to share it with."

"Shelly—"

Afraid of his reaction, she rushed on. "Yesterday I told you I love you. Of course, I realize that it was probably too late. I don't know if you still think there's a chance for us. But if there is, I wanted you to know that when you return from space, I'll be waiting for you." She felt her heart pounding in her chest.

"I don't want you to wait for me, Shelly."

An icy chill hit her spine, and her mouth fell open in shock. She hadn't expected him to be so blunt. In fact, in her heart, she'd truly believed he still loved her.

Shelly was so stunned, she almost didn't hear his next words. It was his broad smile that caught her focus. Why was he so happy to be breaking her heart?

"I won't have to wait. I came here to tell you that you're going into space."

Shelly stared at him as though he had two heads. "You're not making any sense."

"We had an emergency meeting this morning. Colonel Murphy was sold on trying to make the two-man crew idea work. But there were a lot of gaps in the plan. So, I suggested we take a civilian."

She could barely breathe. "Me?"

"That's right, but you're not just any civilian. You designed Draco from its first bolt. You trained on all the simulators before you trained us. You're a licensed pilot, and you know the mission…and all its secrets."

"And they went along with this idea?"

"I convinced them that if they were willing to proceed with no one, you'd be a hell of a lot better than that."

"Thanks a lot," Shelly said, laughing. "But what about Secretary Yates? He hates me. There's no way he'd approve this."

"He was in the meeting. He's had a full load managing this scandal and keeping the true nature of GRM out of the press. He was willing to sign off on whatever was going to get this mission under way. I asked them to let me tell you myself."

She leaned forward to hug him tightly. "Thank you so much. Obviously, none of this would be happening without you." She felt as if she was going to burst.

"You don't have to thank me. You saved my life last night. The main reason I wanted to come see you was to tell you that I still love you. And I believe we can make this work."

Shelly jumped onto his lap, straddling his hips as she pressed her face into his neck. "You don't know how happy I am to hear that," she said softly.

"Probably as happy as I am to say it. We're going to be working together in a whole new way. Monday morning you'll get fitted for your space suit. Then we'll have to leave for Florida, where we'll cram in everything you'll need to know to be my copilot—"

Shelly cut him off with a kiss. "Enough shoptalk. Starting tomorrow, I'm willing to eat, sleep and breathe the mission. But I want to spend today making up for lost time."

With that, she slipped her hands under his NASA polo and tugged it up his torso and over his head. She loved watching each muscle contract as she followed the shirt's path with a light caress of her nails.

"I like the way you think," he said, pushing her off his lap so he could peel her robe off her shoulders.

Before she could register the cool air on her skin, he swung her into his arms and carried her to the bedroom.

As soon as Shelly's feet touched the carpet, their bodies became a blur of motion, each of them grabbing at clothing and tearing it away.

As soon as her skin was exposed, Linc honed in on one spot with tongue flicks and wet kisses. When his clothes fell away, Shelly's hands explored him, her fingertips lightly raking him.

With the two of them finally naked, Shelly's hunger climbed fast, like a rocket shooting through her core. It felt like an eternity since they'd last touched.

His mouth was on hers, drawing her lips to his in long pulls. When they finally separated to fill their lungs with air, the sight of his sculpted body overwhelmed her senses. And she went to her knees.

Finding herself in a prime spot to take advantage of his arousal, Shelly loved him with her mouth.

He was strong and hard and yet velvet soft to her tongue. Her hands found the firm mounds of his backside and held tight for leverage.

As she moved back and forth, lost in this new art, Linc's breath came out in pants. With his head thrown back and his eyes pressed shut, he moaned her name.

Seconds later, he pulled her to her feet and tossed her gently on the bed. Shelly bounced against the rumpled sheets, taking Linc's weight as he covered her.

Soundlessly, his mouth moved from the dip in her throat to the crevice between her breasts. His tongue found first one nipple and then the other, making Shelly's body quake with pleasure.

Trailing wet kisses past her navel, his mouth found her pelvic bones and her sensitive inner thighs. Now she was so worked up, she could barely keep still.

Linc held her in place as his tongue found her most sensitive secret. Her back arched off the bed as he continued to tease her with his lips.

Finally, when she didn't think she could take any more, Linc entered her. Their bodies were fused together, and Shelly knew things were finally as they should be.

His hips rocked against hers in quick thrusts, pushing all coherent thought from her mind. She raised her hips to his, and they were locked in tandem motion.

Blood rushed through her veins, signaling the countdown. Her climax was ready to launch in five…four…three… Linc increased his pace, growling her name with urgency.

Two…one…blast off!

Together, they rocketed to the stars, curled in a steamy embrace.

Epilogue

Linc's ranch was filled with rambunctious kids ranging in age from eight to sixteen. The Wide Open Spaces camp for urban children was in full swing. And Shelly was thrilled to be a part of it.

Today's activities had a country fair theme, with horse-shoe tossing, a small petting zoo, and pie-eating competitions.

"Here you are," Shelly said to a curly-haired girl as she handed her a double scoop of strawberry ice cream. She had asked to man this station to help beat the brutal August heat.

"You weren't kidding about this Houston humidity," Cheryl said, trying to smooth her slowly expanding shoulder-length hair.

Cheryl had come to visit with her kids, who were

happy to help them run the ice-cream station, realizing they'd get plenty of extra scoops for themselves.

Shelly laughed. "I tried to warn you. Around here, hair gel and buns are your friend."

"And yet you stand there, looking as cool as can be. What happened to the queen of hair disasters?"

Shelly tucked a strand of her new short hairdo behind her ear. "Janet happened. She's a hair genius, not to mention she gives free relationship therapy with a shampoo and style."

Janet had cut Shelly's hair to a manageable length, just below her ears. She'd given her a great new relaxer that worked with her hair's natural curl. Now when the humidity tried to wreak havoc with her style, her hair looked as if it was supposed to be that way.

"Well, just look at you," Cheryl said, filling a dish with chocolate ice cream. "Things just couldn't be better. I guess I should be glad that you're still speaking to us peasants now that you're famous."

Guardian Rescue Mission had been successfully completed two months ago, and she and Linc had moved in together as soon as it was over. That was their best chance to spend as much time together as possible. Shelly had been accepted into the astronaut program and was currently a celebrity in her own right.

Word had gotten out that she'd gone into space as a civilian, making her the topic of several news reports and articles. The context of GRM was still a safely guarded secret, but Shelly's astronaut dreams were now a reality.

Not a day went by without Shelly taking the time to cherish a special memory from her amazing journey. The black of space was a color and texture she'd never found on Earth. And the stars were suspended within the layers of clear darkness like hundreds of pinpoints of light on invisible strings.

Looking through the spacecraft's windows at her home, Shelly had marveled at the oceans, thunderstorms that broke across the planet like fireworks and a sunset that framed the earth with layer after layer of unimaginable shades of blue. Although she'd seen some incredible sights, nothing compared to the thrill of the work itself.

Shelly's thoughts returned to earth as Linc, wearing his cowboy hat and a NASA shirt, walked up and stopped in front of their table.

Shelly held up her ice cream scoop. "What flavor would you like?"

"I'm not here for ice cream. I'm here to steal you away for just a second," he said and glanced to Cheryl. "Can you handle this on your own for a few minutes?"

"You two run along," Cheryl said, never breaking her pace. "We've got this covered."

When they were alone in Linc's den, Shelly turned to him, filled with curiosity. "So what's up?"

"Look what came in the mail today," he said, holding out a magazine.

Shelly ripped the *Time* magazine out of his hands. "Oh, my gosh. They gave me the cover. When they did the interview, I never dreamed I'd make the cover."

He laughed. "And here I thought I'd given up dating cover girls."

Shelly held the magazine up, next to her face. "I suppose you'll want me to autograph this for you. Now you're not the only big shot in this house."

Linc pretended to brood. "Well, you still haven't

made *People* magazine. Don't forget I was one of their most eligible bachelors."

She cringed as she looked over at the framed magazine cover on the wall of his den, featuring him with a toothy grin and the caption Mr. Right Stuff.

Shelly punched him in the arm. "And don't *you* forget that you're not eligible anymore."

Linc pulled her into his arms and squeezed her against his chest. "That's right, because pretty soon I'm going to make you *Mrs*. Right Stuff."

*The "Triple Threat" Donovan brothers are back...
and last-man-standing Trent is about to roll the
dice on falling in love.*

Defying DESIRE

Book #3 in *The Donovan Brothers*

A.C. Arthur

When it comes to men, model Tia St. Claire wants no
strings, just flings. But navy SEAL Trent Donovan stirs
defiant longings she can't deny. Happily unattached,
Trent has dedicated his career to duty and danger, until
desire—and Tia—changes everything.

"If hero Adam Donovan was for sale, every woman in
the world would be lined up to buy him!"
—*Romantic Times BOOKreviews* on
A CINDERELLA AFFAIR

*Coming the first week of April 2009
wherever books are sold.*

**KIMANI™
ROMANCE**

www.kimanipress.com
www.myspace.com/kimanipress   KPACA1090409

Her family circle had always been broken…
until now.

Nine
MONTHS
WITH
Thomas

Fan-favorite author

SHIRLEY
HAILSTOCK

For Meghan Howard, Mother's Day has a whole new meaning! After she fulfills an extraordinary agreement with widower Thomas Worthington-Yates, Meghan's prepared to go her own way. But their undeniable attraction has Meghan dreaming of the unthinkable: a future—and a family—together.

Coming the first week of April 2009
wherever books are sold.

KIMANI™
ROMANCE

He's an irresistible recipe—for trouble!

Sugar RUSH

elaine overton

Life is sweet for bakery owner Sophie Mayfield.
She's saved her family business from a takeover, and
hired talented baker Eliot Wright to help sales. Eliot
is as appealing—and oh-so-chocolate-fine—as he is
hardworking. But when Sophie discovers Eliot is not
what he seems, Eliot must regain Sophie's trust—and
prove he's her permanent sweet spot.

*Coming the first week of April 2009
wherever books are sold.*

KIMANI™
ROMANCE

www.kimanipress.com
www.myspace.com/kimanipress   KPEO1110409

REQUEST YOUR FREE BOOKS!

2 FREE NOVELS
PLUS 2 FREE GIFTS!

KIMANI™
ROMANCE

Love's ultimate destination!

YES! Please send me 2 FREE Kimani™ Romance novels and my 2 FREE gifts (gifts are worth about $10). After receiving them, if I don't wish to receive any more books, I can return the shipping statement marked "cancel." If I don't cancel, I will receive 4 brand-new novels every month and be billed just $4.69 per book in the U.S. or $5.24 per book in Canada, plus 25¢ shipping and handling per book and applicable taxes, if any*. That's a savings of over 20% off the cover price! I understand that accepting the 2 free books and gifts places me under no obligation to buy anything. I can always return a shipment and cancel at any time. Even if I never buy another book from Kimani Press, the two free books and gifts are mine to keep forever.

168 XDN EF2D   368 XDN EF3T

Name	(PLEASE PRINT)	
Address		Apt. #
City	State/Prov.	Zip/Postal Code

Signature (if under 18, a parent or guardian must sign)

Mail to The Reader Service:
IN U.S.A.: P.O. Box 1867, Buffalo, NY 14240-1867
IN CANADA: P.O. Box 609, Fort Erie, Ontario L2A 5X3

Not valid to current subscribers of Kimani Romance books.

Want to try two free books from another line?
Call 1-800-873-8635 or visit www.morefreebooks.com.

* Terms and prices subject to change without notice. N.Y. residents add applicable sales tax. Canadian residents will be charged applicable provincial taxes and GST. Offer not valid in Quebec. This offer is limited to one order per household. All orders subject to approval. Credit or debit balances in a customer's account(s) may be offset by any other outstanding balance owed by or to the customer. Please allow 4 to 6 weeks for delivery. Offer available while quantities last.

Your Privacy: Kimani Press is committed to protecting your privacy. Our Privacy Policy is available online at www.eHarlequin.com or upon request from the Reader Service. From time to time we make our lists of customers available to reputable third parties who may have a product or service of interest to you. If you would prefer we not share your name and address, please check here. ☐

KROM08R

A dazzling story of a woman forced to decide where her heart really lies…

AWARD-WINNING AUTHOR

ADRIANNE BYRD

Love
takes time

All her life, Alyssa Jansen has loved handsome, wealthy Quentin Dwayne Hinton—a man who barely knows she exists. Now after years away in France, Alyssa's back, and Q is seeing her in a whole new light. But so is his brother Sterling, a handsome and passionate man who is willing to give Alyssa what she wants. Suddenly Alyssa must choose between a fairy tale come true and a new, unexpected love….

Coming the first week of April 2009 wherever books are sold.

ARABESQUE®

www.kimanipress.com
www.myspace.com/kimanipress

KPAB1170409

National bestselling author

ROCHELLE ALERS

Naughty

Parties, paparazzi, red-carpet catfights…

Wild child Breanna Parker's antics have
always been a ploy to gain attention from
her diva mother and record-producer father.
As her marriage implodes, Bree moves to
Rome. There she meets charismatic Reuben,
who becomes both her romantic and business
partner. But just as she's enjoying her
successful new life, Bree is confronted
with a devastating scandal that threatens
everything she's worked so hard for....

*Coming the first week of March 2009
wherever books are sold.*

KIMANI PRESS™

www.kimanipress.com
www.myspace.com/kimanipress
KPRA1280309

New York Times Bestselling Author

BRENDA JACKSON

invites you to continue your journey
with the always sexy and always satisfying
Madaris family novels....

FIRE AND DESIRE
January 2009

SECRET LOVE
February 2009

TRUE LOVE
March 2009

SURRENDER
April 2009

ARABESQUE®

"The Madaris family is one that fans will never tire of!"
—*Romantic Times BOOKreviews*

NEW YORK TIMES BESTSELLING AUTHOR

BRENDA JACKSON

SURRENDER

A Madaris Family Novel

Military brat Nettie Brooms has vowed never to become involved with a military man. But Ashland Sinclair, a marine colonel, has very different ideas about the sexy restaurant owner. Now Nettie's wondering how a man she swore she would avoid could so easily test her resolve by igniting a passion she can't walk away from.

Available the first week of April 2009 wherever books are sold.

ARABESQUE®

www.kimanipress.com
www.myspace.com/kimanipress

KPBJI360409